FamilyFun
My Great Idea

EDITIONS

NEW YORK

This book is dedicated to the readers of
FamilyFun **magazine.**

FamilyFun
My Great
Idea

**FAMILYFUN
EDITORS**
Deanna F. Cook
Charlotte Meryman

**EDITORIAL
ASSISTANTS**
Jean Cranston
Amy Hamel

COPY EDITOR
Faye Wolfe

**CONTRIBUTING
EDITORS**
Dawn Chipman, Mary
Giles, Ann Hallock,
Alexandra Kennedy,
Gregory Lauzon, Paula
Noonan, and Lisa
Stiepock

**IMPRESS INC.
CREATIVE DIRECTOR**
Hans Teensma

DESIGN DIRECTOR
Carolyn Eckert

PROJECTS DIRECTOR
Lisa Newman

ART ASSOCIATES
Jen Darcy
Katie Winger

Most of the ideas in this book first
appeared in *FamilyFun* magazine.
FamilyFun is a division of the Walt
Disney Publishing Group. To order
a subscription, call 800-289-4849.

The staffs of *FamilyFun* and Impress,
Inc. conceived and produced
FamilyFun My Great Idea at 244
Main Street, Northampton, Massa-
chusetts 01060, in collaboration with
Disney Editions, 114 Fifth Avenue,
New York, New York 10011-5690.

We extend our gratitude to
FamilyFun's many readers who
shared with us the creative ideas
that are featured in this book.

Special thanks to the following
FamilyFun magazine writers for
their contributions: Gigi Amateau,
Rani Arbo, David Austin, Lynne
Bertrand, Sharon Miller Cindrich,
Shelly Coriell, Diane Dodson,
Darcie Gore, Maryellen Kennedy
Duckett, Alice Lesch Kelly, Frederick
G. Levine, Catherine Newman,
Leslie Garisto Pfaff, Lynne Ticknor,
Beth Tomkiw, Denise Vega, and
Pamela Waterman.

This book would not have been
possible without the talented
FamilyFun magazine staff, who
edited and art-directed the material
for the magazine. In addition to
the book staff credited at left, we'd
like to acknowledge the following
staff members: Jonathan Adolph,
Douglas Bantz, Nicole Blasenak,
Kristen Branch, Jodi Butler, Terry
Carr, Barbara Findlen, Grace
Ganssle, Moira Greto, Michael
Grinley, Ginger Barr Heafey, Elaine
Kehoe, Tom Lepper, Cindy A.
Littlefield, Laura MacKay, Mark
Mantegna, Jennifer Mayer, Dana
Stiepock, Adrienne Stolarz, Mike
Trotman, Ellen Harter Wall, Sandra
L. Wickland, and Katharine
Whittemore. We also would like to
thank our partners at Disney
Editions, especially Wendy Lefkon
and Jody Revenson.

ABOUT THE EDITORS:
Deanna F. Cook, Creative
Development Director of
FamilyFun magazine, is the editor
of the *FamilyFun* book series from
Disney Editions, as well as the
author of *The Kids' Multicultural
Cookbook* from Williamson. She
lives in Florence, Massachusetts,
with her husband, Doug, and their
girls, Ella and Maisie.

Charlotte Meryman is a Contributing Editor for *FamilyFun* magazine and the editor of *Parenting
from the Heart*, a publication of
Motherwear International. She lives
in western Massachusetts with her
husband, Ben Thompson, and their
children, Madeline and Sawyer.

ISBN 0-7868-5541-X

First Edition
10 9 8 7 6 5 4 3 2 1

Library of Congress Cataloging-in-
Publication data on file.

Table of Contents

CHAPTER 1

Everyday Magic 8

Daily Routines ▪ Morning Motivators ▪ Getting Dressed ▪ School Day Breakfasts ▪ Home to School Connections ▪ School Lunches ▪ Family Schedules ▪ Taming the TV ▪ Errand Easers ▪ Chore Time ▪ Dinner Menu Planning ▪ Feeding Picky Eaters ▪ Getting Kids to Bed

CHAPTER 2

Family Traditions 52

Special Family Days ▪ Together Time Around Town ▪ Communication Rituals ▪ Family Fitness Traditions ▪ Dinner Table Traditions ▪ Family Nights

CHAPTER 3

Fun Stuff to Do 82

Activity Starters ▪ Fantasy Play ▪ Craft Organizers ▪ Mess-Free Painting ▪ Recycled Crafts ▪ Photo Cutouts ▪ Personalized Games ▪ Games on the Go ▪ Backyard Activities ▪ Welcoming Spring ▪ Summer Activities ▪ Fall Fun ▪ Winter Fun ▪ Learning Fun ▪ Reading & Writing ▪ Geography ▪ Science ▪ Math & Money

CHAPTER 4

Raising Kind Kids 154

Manners ▪ Creative Thank-yous ▪ Teacher Appreciation ▪ Friendship ▪ Family Connections ▪ Community Service

CHAPTER 5

Milestones & Memories 196

Birthday Traditions ▪ Welcoming a New Baby ▪ First Day of School ▪ Family Keepsakes ▪ Vacation Memories

CHAPTER 6

Family Home 222

Controlling Clutter ▪ Kids' Bedrooms ▪ Decorating ▪ Displaying Kids' Artwork ▪ Laundry & Clothing ▪ Bathrooms

Creative Parenting

A playful approach to solving the daily challenges of family life

■ ■

The editors at *FamilyFun* are convinced that every parent has great ideas. Each month, the My Great Idea section of our magazine receives more than 200 letters from families across the country sharing their creative solutions for getting kids to bed on time, managing sibling rivalries, handling the influx of toys, and more. In this book, you'll find our favorites from among the thousands of ideas our readers have sent us.

Turn the page and you'll meet parents who are doers, who like to tackle things head-on, and who are committed to positive parenting. They believe the best solutions are fun not only for kids but for parents, too. Whether it's a chart that gets children interested in doing chores or a trick that helps kids act politely at the dinner table, all the ideas in this book are simple, straightforward, and family-tested.

When we looked at these letters as a whole, we realized there were a few basic principles we could glean. You may find it helpful to keep them in mind as you shape solutions that fit for you.

Put your family first. We live in an over-scheduled world, and each of us is often engrossed in separate activities like soccer practice, play dates, and working extra hours to meet a deadline. Still, it's important to carve out time to be together as a family. Decide where your schedule can give a little — and let it.

Find a family solution. Two (or three or four) heads are better than one. Whether you're choreographing the week's activities or brainstorming ways to get along better, working together to solve problems makes life easier on everyone.

Create rituals. Find a family tradition that works for you. It might be a conversation game you play at dinner, a weekly walk around the block, or a Friday night living-room camp-in — whatever the form, these rituals will bring your family closer.

Help your kids pitch in around the house.
Children really do want to feel like responsible members of the household; they're just not always sure how to go about it. Invite them to cook a special dinner, choose their chores, and craft family keepsakes.

Try a game, activity, or change in routine. Is your child having trouble falling asleep? Sprinkle some invisible magic dust around her room. Do you need help folding the laundry? Suggest a clean clothes relay race. Often, it is the simple diversions that turn around moods and get kids back on track.

Enjoy your time together. Much as it sometimes feels otherwise, childhood really is fleeting. With a sense of humor, a little creativity, and a good dose of joy, you can make the most of it as it flies along — and still get the chores done.

Send Us Your Great Ideas

Inspired to share your own favorite tips? *FamilyFun* would love to hear them! Write to My Great Idea: From Our Readers Editor, *FamilyFun*, 244 Main Street, Northampton, MA 01060 — or send an e-mail to mgied.familyfun@disney.com. Please include a daytime phone number for verification purposes. Photos are welcome but cannot be returned. We will pay you for each letter we print in the magazine. Letters may be edited for length or clarity.

Chapter 1

Everyday Magic

Creative tips for running your household smoothly all day long

■ ■

Children, it seems, come preprogrammed to wander off track, and keeping your family organized takes determination, inspiration, and a hefty dose of creativity. Luckily, those are qualities *FamilyFun* readers seem to have in spades.

In this chapter, you'll find our favorite tried-and-true tips for keeping kids moving in the morning, staying on top of chores and schedules, taming the TV tiger, smoothing bedtime wrinkles and, ultimately, teaching kids to be responsible members of the household. Not every idea will fit every family, but we think you'll find plenty of fun tips that will work for yours, so you can spend less time supervising and more time playing, talking, and enjoying each other's company.

Contents

10 **Daily Routines**

12 **Morning Motivators**

16 **Getting Dressed**

18 **School Day Breakfasts**

20 **Home to School Connections**

24 **School Lunches**

28 **Family Schedules**

30 **Taming the TV**

32 **Errand Easers**

34 **Chore Time**

42 **Dinner Menu Planning**

44 **Feeding Picky Eaters**

46 **Getting Kids to Bed**

A Day in the Life of Me

This photo album of routines keeps a child on track

"As soon as our son, Easton, turned three, we ran into a few roadblocks in his daily routines. I thought that if he could visualize what a typical day entails,

then he would know what to do and expect. **So I took pictures of him doing his daily activities, from getting**

out of bed in the morning to saying his bedtime prayer. I put the photos in an inexpensive album, along with a drawing of a clock telling the approximate time the activity takes place and a brief description of the activity. He loves to look at the pictures of himself. The book has reinforced the importance of his daily responsibilities, and his reading and time-telling."

—**Beth Royals**
RICHMOND, VIRGINIA

Easton's personal picture-book guides him through his day.

Neat Twist
MORNING CHECKLIST

Twelve-year-old Lauren and ten-year-old Michael Foschino of North Massapequa, New York, take their cues from a checklist posted at the top of the stairs. Before heading down for breakfast each morning, they look to be sure they've done everything on the list — including wash up, make their beds, and put dirty clothes in the hamper — all illustrated with magazine pictures.

Pocket Planner

Picture cards illustrate what's on the agenda

"To let my young children, Haley, four, and Dallin, two, who aren't reading yet, know what chores, outings, or events they can expect each day, I came up with an illustrated day-planner.

On index cards, I drew pictures of chores to be done (setting the table, putting clothes away, and the like) as well as fun activities (having a family date, inviting a friend over, doing a project, writing a letter to Grandma). I then put up a fabric wall-hanging that has one slot for each child's cards and a bigger slot for the completed cards.

Haley checks to see what's in store for the day.

At the beginning of each day, I put four to six cards in each child's slot. The kids are always excited to see what they will be doing each day, and the cards are easy for them to understand."

—Angela Judd
ST. GEORGE, UTAH

Read-Aloud Routine

Wake a child gently by sharing a favorite book

"My nine-year-old daughter, Cate, used to wake up in a grumpy mood nearly every school day. I know how much she loves to read, so **one morning I went into her room fifteen minutes before she needed to be up, opened her curtains to let in the morning sun, and began to read to her.** Cate slowly came to life in a bright and cheerful mood! Now I read to her in the morning as well as at night. This time has become very special to both of us. We love deciding together what books to read, and I enjoy a few relaxing moments with my daughter before we both rush into the day."

—**Margaret Shermer**
SUFFOLK, VIRGINIA

Say "Good Morning" with a soothing story.

Quick Tip

HEAT IT UP

Joanie Christian of Colville, Washington, lures her children out from under the covers on cool mornings by tossing their clothes in the dryer for a few minutes to make them toasty warm.

Neat Twist

DOGGY WAKE-UP CALL

Anita Mawer of Simi Valley, California, gave her daughter, Mandy, age twelve, the job of feeding their two dogs. "Our Lab-Dalmatian mix sings for his breakfast. Just one chorus from him and our daughter rouses herself," Anita says.

Personal Soundtrack

Stay on schedule with a recording of tunes and reminders

"To help keep my kindergartner on task in the morning, I recorded her favorite songs on a cassette. **Between the songs, I recorded reminders of what needed to be done next to finish getting ready for school,** such as 'After this song, go eat breakfast' and 'You need to be dressed, including socks and shoes, when this next song is over.'

On the other side of the tape, I recorded another set of songs, along with instructions relating to bedtime. I used more upbeat songs for the morning side of the tape and more mellow music to help her unwind before bedtime. The tape helped Amanda make sure she was always on track, without any nagging from me."

—Tabitha Dingess
FREDERICKSBURG, VIRGINIA

Neat Twist
MUSICAL CHALLENGE

Mary McClennan of Highland Mills, New York, has improved her family's speed and mood in the morning by challenging herself to have breakfast on the table and her six- and seven-year-old sons to be dressed and seated by the end of a specific tune.

Put a Timer in Charge

An alarm tells kids to finish up breakfast

Cassie, age nine, and Nicky, five, are dawdlers when it comes to dining, says mom **Julie Carlisle,** a third-grade teacher from **Pompano Beach, Florida.** "I felt like I spent the whole morning going, 'Eat! Eat!'" she says. **So she began setting the kitchen timer to go off 15 minutes before it was time to leave and telling the children that when it rang, breakfast was over.**

This simple trick changed everything by taking Mom out of the equation. Suddenly, says Julie, "I wasn't the bad guy. I wasn't the one telling them, 'Hurry up! Hurry up!'" Now, she says, Nicky loves to let her know, "Mommy, I beat the clock!"

Customized Clock

Adding pictures of activities helps even young children know when it's time to do what

"After a wake-up battle on our son's second day of kindergarten, we all agreed we needed a new approach to the day. **We decided to change the face of the clock and make it understandable for a five-year-old.** We placed a sun at the wake-up hour — 7 A.M. — sewed a miniature pair of pants and glued them on at ten minutes after, used a magnet of eggs at twenty minutes past, and a toothbrush at thirty minutes past. He now understands and takes care of his responsibilities in a timely manner, and he is enthused to be in charge of his own schedule."

—Donna Alms and Michael Strauss
WAIKOLOA, HAWAII

Neat Twist
MOCK CLOCK
Priscilla Johnson of Tigard, Oregon, photocopied her kitchen clock with the hands set on the time her first-grader, Joel, needs to leave to catch the school bus. Then she mounted the copy on construction paper and tacked it to their bulletin board, next to the working clock, so Joel can compare the two.

Choose a Week's Worth of Outfits

Five-day plan ends morning squabbles

As a kindergartner, Mary Kate Emmerich once refused to get off the bus at school because she hated the shirt she was wearing. The driver had to carry her in. "I was mortified," says mom Debbie, of Lynbrook, New York. She quickly instituted a new, more successful dressing system for Mary Kate and her little brother, Johnny.

Each child decorated **five blank labels with the days of the week and stuck them on a set of hangers. Every Sunday, the kids (with final sign-off from Debbie) set up their outfits for the week** with the understanding that what they pick, they have to wear.

Neat Twist

CLOTHES CLONE

Each night, Hannah and Mackenzy Derrick of Rock Springs, Wyoming, lay out the next day's clothes on the floor in the shape of a person (including everything from socks to hair accessories). Whatever their "Clothes Kid" wears to sleep, they wear to school the next day. The result? A big reduction in the number of fits thrown, says mom Kandi.

Firefighters' Muster

Kids organize their outerwear so they can race out the door

"The last five minutes before leaving for school in the morning were often harried in our house, especially in the winter. Getting outerwear on was nerve-racking, and a misplaced mitten or boot added to the chaos. Then we visited a local fire hall, and the kids saw how the firefighters keep their turnout gear beside the truck so they can rapidly prepare for an emergency. Impressed, we decided to try this at home. **Each night, the kids ready their 'gear': boots are lined up by the door with snow pants on top of them, hat on pants, and coat behind. The backpack stands ready to strap on last. When I announce, 'Let's go!' the kids scramble to get ready,** and mornings run much more smoothly. And if it sounds like a game for boys, we're a family with three daughters!"

—Tracy Haslam

WHITBY, ONTARIO, CANADA

Turn the chore of putting on winter gear into a game.

Set Up a Buffet

When everything is laid out in advance, kids can easily help themselves

Before leaving early for work, **David Vining** of **Winston-Salem, North Carolina,** sets the table for breakfast, puts a vitamin at each child's place, and leaves out a selection of cereal, muffins, fruit, and other goodies. **When his four daughters (ages two to nine) come down to eat, they serve themselves from his buffet using small pitchers of milk and juice filled and refrigerated the night before.**

Mom Birdie Lynn uses the breakfast break to get herself ready for the day. David's contribution helps tremendously, she says: "Whereas it only takes him five minutes to put it out, it probably saves me twenty in serving it."

Neat Twist
BREAKFAST IN BED

Every weekday morning, David and Emily Rose Chabot, ages seven and four, of Rockland, Massachusetts, snuggle in bed with Dad while mom Paula gets a simple breakfast together on a folding wooden tray. Then the kids eat in bed, chatting with their parents as Mom and Dad get dressed and ready for work. The tradition "helps us spend some peaceful time together before the rush," says Paula.

Breakfast Box

Cut paper in food shapes for a menu kids can handle

"Deciding what to have for breakfast each morning had become a time-consuming task for my children, Nicholas and Courtney, ages eight and six respectively, so I thought of a great way to help them choose quickly and effortlessly. **I cut shapes of various breakfast options from colored paper, including a fried egg and a bowl of oatmeal, and put them all in a box.** Now selecting what they'd like to eat from the breakfast box is a favorite part of their morning routine."

—Shelly Laschkewitsch

LA SELVA BEACH, CALIFORNIA

Toast, fruit, cereal — all are there for the choosing.

Neat Twist

MORNING MENUS

To make weekday mornings a little less harried, Jennifer Glynn of Tucson, Arizona, created menu checklists that her three oldest children, ages three-and-a-half to seven, fill out the night before to place orders for breakfast. The menus offer several types of juice, cereal, and fruit, as well as bagels, toast, or waffles with syrup.

After-School Icons

Stick-on symbols head children in the right direction

"My son Nate, age seven, started kindergarten with a hectic afternoon schedule. He went to day care after school two days a week, I picked him up one day, and he rode the bus home the other two days. **To help him and his teachers adjust to his changing routine, I created little signs to attach to his backpack picturing the routes he would use.** I made the signs on white cardboard, sealed them in plastic sleeves, and attached Velcro tabs to the back. Each morning he attaches the appropriate sign to his backpack."

Velcro reminders tell Nate and little brother Justin how they're getting home.

—**Sandie Smialek**
GIRARD, PENNSYLVANIA

Neat Twist
BACKPACK NOTES

To remind her children of things they need to take to school that can't be packed the night before, Beth Obergh of Wantagh, New York, clips notes to her kids' backpacks with a wooden clothespin marked with their name. "I always put it on the open part of the zipper, so they can't close the backpack with the clothespin on, and it's really obvious," Beth says.

Make Up a Memory Phrase

A silly sentence helps one child stay organized

Nalina Sivagurunathan of **Portage, Michigan,** was tired of having her daughter arrive home from school minus her coat, or her lunch box . . . or her homework folder. **So she invented a funny sentence, using some of her daughter's favorite things, for Neevetha, age eight, to recite as a checklist.** "Cats Love Big Fish" prompted Neevetha to bring home her coat, lunch box, backpack, and folder.

Nalina has also used such personalized sentences — both in English and in her native Tamil — to help Neevetha memorize the colors of the rainbow, the planets, and the order of mathematical symbols.

Remembering school gear is easy with a simple catchphrase.

Draft a Form Letter

A few quick checks give teachers all the info

A professional organizer by trade, **Ruthann Betz-Essinger** of **Vestavia Hills, Alabama,** has worked her magic on her own mornings. Among her inspirations is **a form letter for sending quick notes to her sons' teachers. Drafted on a home computer, the note features boxes Ruthann checks off** to indicate things such as whether Kenton, age ten, or Jackson, eight, is riding in a car pool or leaving early for some reason. There's also an "other" category for comments such as, "The spots on his face are not contagious!"

"The teachers seem to like it because it's just exactly what they need to know — no more, no less — and they can look at it quickly," says Ruthann. "I always sign it and include my cell-phone number — and I handwrite that part, so the teacher knows it's me."

Checked boxes make these notes a breeze for parents to send — and teachers to read.

Knapsack Neatener

Get the message through with these tubular couriers

"We were tired of opening our six- and four-year-old sons' school knapsacks and finding crumpled-up notes, ragged artwork, and water-stained school calendars. Last winter, a pair of wet mittens even destroyed one boy's prized painting. To solve this problem, **we turned Pringles potato chip canisters into carrying tubes for important papers.** We cleaned and dried the empty cylinders, then affixed decorative Con-Tact paper to the outsides. Rolled up sideways, notes and artwork now arrive home dry and wrinkle-free."

Philippe and William keep it clean with their school-paper carriers.

—Cynthia Rankin

PETERBOROUGH, ONTARIO, CANADA

Healthy Eating

Use the rainbow to pack a balanced meal

"Whether we're off to play school or picnic in the park, my three- and five-year-old daughters are responsible for packing their own lunches. To assure that they put together a healthy meal, **I have them make a Rainbow Lunch. They have to pack an assortment of different-colored foods,** such as purple yogurt, red strawberries, orange carrots, and yellow bananas (we've even added blue food coloring to milk for fun). All I have to do is make a sandwich for each. The girls get plenty of fruits and veggies in their colorful lunches, and since they choose the menu, they don't complain about what they're eating."

—Robin Hurwitz

SAN JOSE, CALIFORNIA

Neat Twist

WRITTEN RECORD

Liz Ruff of West Chester, Pennsylvania, didn't want to get into the classic morning debate over who would take what for lunch. So she asked her sons to post a list of favorite foods on the fridge. The boys agreed to eat what their mom packs, as long as it's on the list.

Let the Kids Budget Money

Buying or packing lunch — the decision is up to the children

With school lunches eating up a big slice of the weekly budget, it was impossible for the Stantons of Liberty Center, Ohio, to give their five kids allowances. So Lisa Stanton decided to **allot each child $10 weekly and let him or her choose to pay for school lunches or keep the cash and pack lunches from home.**

Pay for school lunches — or keep the cash and pack lunches from home.

The Lyters of Landisburg, Pennsylvania, devised the same system for Amber, age twelve, only **her $10 also has to pay for lunch fixings.** Says Amber's mom, Lisa, "She takes her time at the grocery store now, comparing store brands versus name brands on price and nutritional values. This plan has taught her more than we originally intended."

Mystery Treat

Wrap up a surprise in your child's lunchbox

"For fun, I sometimes include a Mystery Treat in my son's lunch. It might be a familiar snack, like chocolate chips, a new food he has never tried, such as pistachios, or something just a little unusual, like gummy sharks. **I wrap the treat in aluminum foil to disguise it and attach a clue to the outside, so Trent, age ten, can try to guess what the treat is before he opens it.** The Mystery Treats have become a lunchtime hit with Trent and his friends."

—Jill Hibbard
INTERLOCHEN, MICHIGAN

Neat Twist
BAG LUNCH WITH A PRIZE

On rainy days, Alicia Ebert of Woodruff, South Carolina, serves her two sons homemade kids' meals for lunch. She gives Lewis, six, and Austin, four, each a brown paper lunch bag to decorate. Then, she places their food order in their bags along with a toy (stickers, Play-Doh, or a Matchbox car, for example).

Lunchtime Laughs

One-a-day pages offer a double dose of humor

"Last year, our family received as holiday gifts two **day-by-day calendars with tear-off pages. They were filled with funny cartoons and clever quotes,** and rather than throw away pages as the days passed, we came up with better uses for them. **When I pack the kids' lunches, I toss one in** (I always cut off the dates). We get twice the laughs, plus my kids learn a lesson about reusing and recycling."

—Karen Jameson
VALENCIA, CALIFORNIA

Neat Twist

NAPKIN OF THE DAY

Each day, Rivana Stadtlander of Aventura, Florida, tucks a different playful party napkin into her daughter's lunchbox. The tradition started accidentally when Rivana ran out of plain napkins. Now, she maintains her supply by watching for sales and stocking up on themes dear to Alivia's heart.

Create Daily Flip Cards

A fridge flip book helps one family keep it together

For **Pam Widdoes,** the hardest part of having three daughters in three different classes is remembering who needs gym clothes or a musical instrument on which day. So the **Mount Laurel, New Jersey,** mom made a simple set of flip cards to hang on the fridge. **Each white index card is labeled at the top with a day of the week. Below that is each girl's name, her special activities and the items required, color-coded by child.** The cards are hole-punched in one corner, bound with a key ring, and hooked over a magnetic clothespin on the refrigerator.

Color-coded index cards provide a simple daily reference.

Neat Twist
COLOR-CODED CALENDAR
The Daffrons of Ramsey, New Jersey, keep track of who's where when with a Day Runner calendar, which is displayed handily on the refrigerator (and includes a pocket for keeping markers within reach). Each family member has chosen his or her own color and a corresponding marker for writing in appointments, practices, days off, and other notable events. The result: schedules that virtually pop off the wall so new plans can be easily organized and those made earlier aren't forgotten and missed.

Daily Triage

A quick purge keeps school papers under control

"When my son gets off the bus, **I go through his book bag immediately and enter new stuff in my week-at-a-glance day planner — and throw out that paper immediately.** That way everything is in one place. By doing it right away, I drastically reduce 'The Pile.'"

— Lynn Schumaker

NORTHWOOD, OHIO

Transferring information to your calendar each day keeps things from stacking up.

Quick Tip

MEET WEEKLY

Each Sunday after supper, the Osleys of Bolton, Connecticut gather to go over the week's activities. This simple review makes for fewer surprises on busy days, like forgotten sports equipment or sudden science projects.

Tickets for the Tube

Daily coupons limit television time

Homemade tickets keep track of time in front of the TV.

"I came up with a great way to help my six-year-old daughter, Veronica, limit the amount of time she spends watching television. **Every morning I give her four TV tickets, each one good for half an hour.** She turns one in for each half-hour show that she watches, and when she runs out of tickets, she's done watching for the day. **Leftover tickets are saved up and traded in for new books** (one for every five tickets). My daughter is cutting her own TV time and improving her reading skills in the process."

—Kim Zea

SANTA CLARA, CALIFORNIA

Neat Twist

TOKEN TRADE-OFF

Every Sunday or Monday, the Bakers of Wagoner, Oklahoma, hand out five tokens worth 30 minutes of TV time to each of their kids. The kids (three girls ages six through twelve) write their choices on the calendar and "pay" before the show starts. The girls also can pool their tokens to watch a movie or save them up and cash them in at the end of the week for 25 cents apiece. The payoff? The kids are choosier about TV and are reading more, says mom Traci — and the family spends more real time together.

Create a Fun Zone

A truly special play space gives TV a run for its money

To lure Aaron, age eleven, and Brandon, seven, away from the television, **Tara Yerkie** of **Hartly, Delaware, transformed their little-used dining room into a special area where her sons could get creative.** She filled a bunch of shelves with their books, games, and puzzles, and added a radio with a cassette deck. Tara also brought in cabinets with drawers for craft supplies and put a plastic tablecloth over the dining room table. Oh, and one other thing: she canceled the family's cable TV service. Now, instead of vegging out, she says, the kids can often be found building with Lincoln Log pieces or playing a game.

Where-We're-Going Map

Spice up humdrum outings with an illustrated itinerary

"I came up with a way to help my sons, Austin, age eight, and Brandon, six, have some fun with the otherwise dull task of running errands. **I make each of them an itinerary, complete with check boxes next to small pictures representing each stop,** such as a dollar sign for the bank and a stamped envelope for the post office. I'll even add a surprise stop at the ice-cream parlor, represented by an ice-cream cone hidden under a piece of an index card, for our final stop. Austin and Brandon have fun trying to guess the destination each symbol stands for and marking off the boxes as we complete our tasks."

—**Laurel Burton**

BRIGHAM CITY, UTAH

Quick Tip

PERPETUAL LIST

The Pfaffs of Nutley, New Jersey typed into their computer a list of every grocery item they typically buy, organized to reflect the supermarket's layout. Once a week, they simply print out the list and highlight what they need. Their daughter, Lily, marks her requests (which are considered discretionary) in another color.

The Coupon Game

Turn a trip to the supermarket into a fun search

"I used to shudder when I thought about taking my two- and six-year-old sons to the grocery store with me. The boys invariably were fighting with each other, not to mention squishing the bread and breaking the eggs. Then I came up with a game — match the coupon — to make these trips fun, a little educational, and a lot easier. **I give my older son, Dalton, the coupons for the aisle we are in, and he finds the products by matching the pictures.** For each, we compare the unit cost to that of store brands, and I let him figure out which is cheaper. Then Clayton takes the items and puts them in the cart. Both stay happy and occupied and learn a little about economics and saving money."

Challenge your kids to match the coupon to the product at the grocery store.

—Nicole McDowell

RUSSELLVILLE, MISSOURI

Bingo Board

When it comes to tasks, prizes can come into play

"To make chores easier (and more fun) for my children, we use personalized bingo charts listing various tasks. **Anthony, age nine, and Julianne, four, each pick the chores they will do, and we place a sticker on the chart over each task when it's completed.** I also add in special squares like "caught sharing" or "doing a good deed." For each bingo they get before the week is up, **they earn Bingo Bucks certificates,** which they save up and then trade for activities or privileges, such as a trip to the movies or vacation spending money. This system gives our kids some power and choice over their chores, which makes things easier for us all."

Bingo cards make for a winning chore solution.

—**Carol Scalise**
TEMECULA, CALIFORNIA

A Punch Card for Chores

This family's chore solution is full of holes

"To help my kids, Kraig, age eight, and Reed, three, stay motivated during the lazy days of summer, I give them each a punch card, for which **they earn holes made with a hole punch whenever they do something on the 'punch-card list,' such as getting dressed, brushing their teeth and making their beds** without being asked more than once, emptying the garbage, and cleaning their rooms. Holes can also be earned for activities such as reading or journal-writing. They even get surprise punches as rewards for random acts of kindness that Mom or Dad catches them doing. Once their cards are full, they get a small toy or book."

—Kristina Farrar
ALBANY, OREGON

Neat Twist
TASK TRAIN

Janet Davis of Ellensburg, Washington, cut craft foam in the shape of train cars to create daily reminders for her kids. Each car lists one task, pulled by an engine bearing the child's name. The trains are laid out on the counter, and as Kurt, age ten, and Kate, seven, complete their chores, they turn over the cars. When all have been flipped, they earn free time.

Post a List of Jobs for Hire

A chart helps kids learn how to earn — and clean house

Stephanie Curley of **North Attleboro, Massachusetts,** uses friendly economic competition to prompt Alex, age eight, and Michael, six, to do chores. Instead of assigning specific jobs to each, **she posts a list of available chores and their wages ("putting away laundry = 25 cents" or "vacuuming = a dollar").** To choose a chore — and they can opt to do none — they simply write in their initials. On payday, Stephanie totals each boy's earnings and gives him his due. Putting the choice in their hands has not only cut down on grumbling, she reports, but has also motivated Alex and Michael to do more. As the initials start filling in, the boys vie for the tasks that will make one of them the week's top breadwinner.

Neat Twist
SWEET REWARDS

For each day that Marissa, age nine, Jesse, five, and Hope, three, complete their assigned tasks, Ruth Gill of Cheney, Washington, adds one dry ingredient of a cookie recipe, such as flour or sugar, to a large, covered bowl. Once all of the nonperishable ingredients are there — usually after about six or seven days — they bake a batch of cookies as a reward.

"Whoops" Board

A quick note alerts kids to overlooked duties

"I posted a small dry-erase in my kitchen and wrote 'WHOOPS!' at the top in big letters. Now when I notice that one of my kids, Cooper, age seven, or Lilliana, nine, didn't do something I asked, such as put away a toy or take a dish into the kitchen, **I simply write his or her initial and a short message describing the 'whoops' on the board.** The next time either one wants me to do something — such as play a board game or make a snack — I say, 'Sure, as soon as you take care of your "whoops."' This system means I don't have to constantly repeat my requests, and they get done without a big fuss."

—Elizabeth White Koebsell

FORESTVILLE, CALIFORNIA

Quick Tip

DOOR SIGN

To keep her daughter's friends from stopping by at inopportune times — like when chores need doing — Mary Stefani of Saline, Michigan, bought two foam door hangers — one green and one red. When Nora, age seven, is free to play, she hangs the green one on the front door. When she's not, she puts out the red one.

A Prize Jar

The luck of the draw makes routine tasks more exciting

"It seemed like I was constantly asking my eight-year-old daughter, Caroline, to pick up her room, make her bed, and take a shower. I tried a money reward system, star stickers, everything. Then I found a way to expand on a system being used in her class at school. **I made up several chore passes with phrases like 'no making your bed today,' 'stay up late,' or 'one free paperback book'** and placed them all in a jar. Caroline has to do her chores for two weeks before **she gets to pick a coupon out of the jar.** This system has really motivated her, and she likes the sense of control she has now."

—**Melissa Harrell**
CHARLOTTE, NORTH CAROLINA

Neat Twist
SPECIAL DISPENSATION

To give her children a little flexibility and control, Jennifer Prindle of Henrietta, New York, created coupons that allow the kids to break the house rules once in a while. On slips of paper she wrote out permission to skip music practice, for example, or have a junk-food dinner. Each child gets just a few coupons per year, and as a result, Jennifer says, "they're very careful about when they use them."

Clean Clothes Relay

Kids learn to fold laundry with this fun game

"When my six children were young, I invented this game to get them to help fold their clothes. Each child is assigned a laundry basket and chooses a corner of the room to put it in. The clean clothing is placed in a pile in the center of the room. **When I say 'go,' they run to the pile and choose three articles of their own clothing, then take them back to their corner, fold them neatly, and place them in a basket.** Each child keeps going until none of his or her clothes are left in the pile. To keep things from getting sloppily folded, I award small prizes, including Neatest Basket and First Done. We have also played a variation in which the kids hop to the pile and walk backward to their basket."

—Barbara Kneeppel
GASPORT, NEW YORK

Get kids to help fold with this racing challenge.

Neat Twist
LAUNDRY LESSON

To help interest her nine-year-old son, Colin, in washing his own clothes, Kari Kjesbo of Norcross, Minnesota, invited him to create his own book: *Colin's Kids' Guide to Doing the Laundry*. As Kari gave the lessons, Colin wrote and illustrated the instructions. When he was done, they took his work to a copy center and had it turned into his very own book.

Table-Setting Tasks

Hand out the jobs to make dinnertime easier

"To help smooth out our harried mealtimes, we implemented Task Place Cards for dinnertime. **Each person, including Mom and Dad, gets a 4- by 6-inch index card decorated with stickers and labeled with a responsibility.** Whoever has the card labeled utensils, for example, takes care of setting the table ahead of time, while the person with the refrigerator card is in charge of retrieving anything needed from the fridge during the meal. Other responsibilities include answering the telephone and the door. We keep one card blank as a freebie, and the cards are rotated each night so no one feels like he is always stuck with the same job."

— Margaret Tindol
BEEVILLE, TEXAS

Neat Twist
PERFECT PLACE MATS

Inspired by an idea she saw in *FamilyFun,* Joan Blodgett of Corapolis, Pennsylvania, used construction-paper place mats to help her four-year-old son, Logan, learn how to set the table. The mats feature colored shapes showing where to place the plate, cup, and utensils, and are laminated with clear Con-Tact paper for repeat use.

Place Cards with a Twist

Simple chore lists offer just the right amount of direction

"I have found a great way to keep my two children, ages ten and thirteen, moving at the end of the day, when they still have chores to do but are beginning to lose their momentum. **On small index cards, I write everything they need to do,** such as put away laundry, pick up their rooms, or get their outfits and backpacks ready for the next day. **I then put each child's card at his or her place at the table.** After dinner, they each take their note card and go off to do what's on the list, checking off each item as they go along. It allows them to do everything at their own pace, and they don't have to keep asking me what else needs to be done."

—Susan Geyer

MILFORD, DELAWARE

Set up a Rotating Menu

Three-week schedule makes meal planning automatic

After reading that the average family has two dozen favorite meals they eat over and over, **Karen Stowe** of **Norfolk, Virginia, sat down to list her family's top fare and came up with a total of 21 entrées.** Realizing she had three weeks' worth of dishes, she created a simple dinner roster, which she follows in order.

After she prepares supper number 21, for instance, she just starts again at the top of the list.

Summer is the time to try out new dishes; the best are added to the list come September. And because everybody hungers for a little variety, Karen builds in an occasional free night for "something totally different" (such as Chinese takeout).

Using the family's favorite recipes to create a revolving menu assures everyone's happy come suppertime.

Recipe File of Favorites

Following cards in order offers an easy supper plan

"Instead of spending time each day figuring out what to make for dinner, **I have collected more than three hundred of my family's favorite main dish recipes and put them in a recipe box.** Each morning, I look at the first recipe in the box, and if I have all the ingredients, I make that for dinner. Afterward, I put that recipe at the back of the box. If I don't have all the necessary items, I put what's missing on the grocery list and continue on through the cards until I find one I can make that evening. After my next grocery shopping trip, I start with the recipes I set aside. Of course, I am flexible if we just feel like having chili dogs or pizza."

—Charlotte J. Parcels
LAKE ZURICH, ILLINOIS

Neat Twist

DECISION DAY

Every Sunday, the Scifords of Omaha, Nebraska, gather in the living room and draw names from a basket. As each is announced, that family member gets to say what they would like for dinner one night of the week. It can be anything, says mom Heather, "as long as it's a balanced meal." The system means everyone has at least one favorite dish to look forward to every week.

Fruit and Veggie Bingo

This game makes healthy eating more fun

"To encourage my son, Justin, age five, to eat more fruits and vegetables, we play Fruit and Veggie Bingo. **We use bingo-style scorecards covered with pictures of fruits and vegetables. Each time he eats one, we mark that box with an X.** When he has eaten a whole row of fruits or veggies, he gets a small prize or healthy treat. Thanks to our bingo game, Justin has enjoyed sampling some new foods and is learning to make good nutrition choices."

—Christine Crytzer

PITTSBURGH, PENNSYLVANIA

Justin shows off his new-foods bingo card.

Quick Tip

COOL IT

Micha Van Cleave of Placerville, California, has her sons, Talen, age six, and Jerin, four, cool their hot cereal — and get some extra nutrition — by mixing in frozen fruit, such as raspberries, peaches, and strawberries.

An Adventurous Eater

A creative food chain turns a picky eater on to new foods

"Our son, Matthew, age six, would refuse to try new foods, gagging and choking whenever he did. Inspired by Eric Carle's book *The Very Hungry Caterpillar,* we came up with a fun way to get Matthew to eat different things. **We cut various colored circles from construction paper, then drew a face on one of them and posted it on the kitchen wall to start a caterpillar.** Every time Matthew tried a new food, we wrote it on one of the circles and added it to the wall. His whole attitude about trying new foods has since changed, and now his caterpillar is winding all around the kitchen."

—Terri Jenkins

YORKTOWN, VIRGINIA

Nightly Check-off

Chart a course for an easy-to-follow bedtime routine

"Tired of always nagging our five-year-old son, Ethan, to get ready for bed, we came up with a way to give him responsibility for the nightly tasks himself. **We purchased an inexpensive write-on/wipe-off board and created a column for each task, headed by an image** (we used computer clip art) to represent it. For example, we selected pictures of a toothbrush, hands (for handwashing), and books (for picking out his bedtime stories). He was so excited to complete each task and check it off with an erasable marker each night that we didn't have to prod him a bit."

—Dawn LaFontaine
ASHLAND, MASSACHUSETTS

Mission: Lights Out

Undercover assignments add a thrill to bedtime chores

"My husband and I have come up with an activity we call Spy Kid to get our children, Jenna, age ten, and Erin, eight, ready for bed without any fuss. **First, we turn out the lights upstairs and give them each a flashlight. Their mission is to sneak upstairs quietly and brush their teeth, use the bathroom, and put on their pajamas.** Then they must quietly retrieve a predetermined toy from their bedroom and deliver it to us without waking up their younger brother, Jack. If they can do all of this successfully, each retains the title of Spy Kid."

A flashlight and a fun mission helps kids get ready for bed without a fuss.

—Sharon Weinberger

ANDOVER, MINNESOTA

Bedtime Paper Chain

A link a day helps keep crankiness away

"When my son, Adam, was having trouble sleeping in his own bed at age two, we started a paper chain that hung from the ceiling above his bed. **Each night that he went to sleep without fussiness, we added a link to his chain. After every ten links, he could choose a new toy!** After twenty-five links, he was sleeping in his own bed and had forgotten the whole purpose of the colorful paper chain that still hangs from his ceiling."

A paper reward chain helped Adam settle in his own bed.

—Pamelyn Cunning

FORT COLLINS, COLORADO

Magic Mommy Dust

Disperse fears with a quick sprinkle

"In my house, Magic Mommy Dust solves all kinds of problems. For instance, **whenever one of my kids, Josh, age nine, or Claire, six, has trouble falling asleep at night or is afraid of something, such as monsters under the bed, I reach into my pocket for some invisible magic dust.** I sprinkle it around the room, under the bed, and on his or her face while saying, 'Magic Mommy Dust, work your magic!' It soothes their fears immediately. I've even put it in coat pockets before school when one of them has needed a little extra assurance. After many applications of Magic Mommy Dust, we all now believe in its power to make everyone feel safe and loved."

—Vicky DeCoster

PAPILLION, NEBRASKA

Neat Twist
ANGEL TRAILS
Each night, after her three children fall asleep, Seema Gersten of North Hollywood, California, sneaks in and leaves a tiny drop of powder glitter on their windowsills. In the morning, the kids are excited to find the glittery trail, left by the angels of their evening prayer, who watch over the sleeping.

Monstrous Sounds

A guessing game eases nighttime fears

"My three-year-old daughter, Katie, refused to sleep in her own bed because of 'scary monster sounds.' The next day, **I used ordinary household objects, such as spoons, paper bags, shoes, and cabinet doors, to make various noises from another room,** asking her, 'What do you think made that noise?' Then she took a turn making the noises as I guessed. Over the next few days, I pointed out other sounds, such as the ticking of the clock and a car's backfire. Now at bedtime Katie proclaims, 'Don't worry, Mommy. That's not a monster, it's only the wind.'"

— **Penny Gene Taub**
LARGO, FLORIDA

Neat Twist
SOUNDER SNOOZING

When stormy nights make sleeping a challenge for her four-year-old daughter, Tracey Sorenson of Menomonie, Wisconsin, has Madeline put on her "bearmuffs" — her favorite stuffed bears. Having her pals snuggled around her head both comforts her and muffles the noise. "Whenever she puts them on, she can doze right off!" says Tracey.

Hug and Kiss Jar

Limit long goodnights with numbered coupons

"Briar's bedtime routine always included stories, hugs, and kisses. But he would constantly summon my husband and me back to his room for even more hugs and kisses. While I never mind showing my son affection, I realized he was using this as a stall tactic to keep from going to sleep. So we developed the Hug and Kiss Jar. I wrote the numbers one through ten on pieces of construction paper, one per square, folded them, and put them in a jar by his bed. **After we've read the last story, Briar, age three, chooses a square from the jar and that's the number of hugs and kisses we share.** He now looks forward to selecting his nightly number and no longer calls us back to his room. It helps him with number recognition and counting, too!"

—Kerri Lehman
DALTON, OHIO

Chapter 2

Family Traditions

How can you bring your family closer? Try these special family days, dinner table traditions, and weekend rituals

■ ■

FamilyFun **contributing editor** Catherine Newman has been reading Mem Fox's *Time for Bed* to Ben, her four-year-old, since he was born. She says her nightly reading is far more than a habit: this simple ritual calls her family together from the apartness of their busy days; it makes their home feel sacred and full night after night.

These qualities define everyday traditions — family rituals that give joy and meaning to the most ordinary daily activities, and that will provide the stuff of some of our children's fondest memories.

On the following pages, you'll find dozens of traditions from *FamilyFun* readers. They don't require that you have more time, more money, or elaborate props. Rather, they invite you to turn the simple moments of life into the special occasions they truly are.

Contents

54 Special Family Days

60 Together Time Around Town

62 Communication Rituals

66 Family Fitness Traditions

68 Dinner Table Traditions

74 Family Nights

Happy Relationship Day

Plan one-on-one time with each of your kids

"With six children all under the age of eleven, it's a struggle to make special time for each one. I've found a wonderful way to turn one day a year into a tribute to the unique and special relationship I have with each child: I call it our 'Relationship Birthday.' First, **each child picks a date other than his or her actual birthday and gets to plan a whole day of activities with me.** Some have chosen to go hiking, others to stay in pajamas all day and play board games, or to make sundaes after a long bike ride. We always end our day with a big birthday cake and candles, one for each year we've known each other. We blow them out together and make a wish."

—Ginny Bishop

LITTLETON, COLORADO

Boss for the Day

Try giving each child a turn to run the show

"Every month, my two kids and I sit down at the kitchen table with the calendar in front of us. **I let them each pick two days during the month, and I mark their names on those dates on the calendar. These become 'their days,' on which they get to choose what we do (within reason!).** We've had lots of fun visiting local parks and farms, painting our faces, eating at ice-cream shops, riding bikes, going to museums, and more. We typically end the day with a pizza party and a movie. It's fun for all of us, and both of the kids love being the boss for the day."

—Karen Lisborg

ROCHESTER, NEW YORK

To celebrate being top dogs for a day, Paul, five, and Emily, seven, chose to don puppy-dog face paint.

Neat Twist

KID OF THE DAY: A SIBLING RIVALRY SOLUTION

The Coriells of Tempe, Arizona, have assigned each of their three daughters two days a week to be in charge of simple decisions, such as what music they listen to, who gets into the car first, and what TV show they watch. For example, Katelyn, age four, is Kid of the Day on Tuesdays and Fridays. On those days, she also is responsible for extra chores that crop up, such as putting away groceries or setting the table. Sundays are Parents' Choice Days, when Mom and Dad call the shots.

Brotherly Love

August 5 is their own day to give thanks for siblings

"After observing Mother's Day and Father's Day, my son, Joshua, age six, wondered why we celebrate those special occasions but not Brother's Day. **I told him if he and his brother Jacob, four, wanted to pick a date, we'd make it an official holiday in our house.** They decided on August 5. Each year, the boys make each other cards or posters and buy a small gift with money they've saved. We all do some special activity together such as going to the zoo or taking a train ride, and end the day with a favorite dinner and dessert. It's been a wonderful way to draw attention to the bond they have."

—**Dawn Kochniarczyk**

GENEVA, ILLINOIS

Jacob and Joshua share a homemade holiday.

Neat Twist

SISTER BOOK

In addition to inventing their own sibling holiday, Christina and Elizabeth Tarjan of Milwaukee, Wisconsin, have created a book to honor it. The Tarjans' Sister Day tome includes pictures they've drawn of each other, along with their ideas about what makes sisters special. They add to the contents each year; they've written about their favorite expressions, colors, movies, and songs, and their similarities and differences. Says mom Jean, "When asked what their favorite holiday is, both now answer 'Sister Day!'"

Pick a Day to Say Yes

One Saturday a month, special requests are the order of the day in this family

Darcy Gore of Paso Robles, California, was tired of telling her kids no. When her girls, seven-year-old Torri, four-year-old Kennedy, and two-year-old Cassidy, would ask "Can you draw with me?" "Will you bake cookies tonight?" "Can we all play Go Fish?" Darcy often found herself saying, "No, not now." So she decided to designate one Saturday a month as Yes Day. **On the days when she says no because she's too busy, Darcy has the girls write their idea on a piece of paper and put it into the Yes Day Jar. Then, on Yes Day, they pull some of the papers out of the jar and do as many of those fun things as they have time for.** Darcy says, "Instead of whining when I tell them no, they ask, 'Will you put it in the Yes Day Jar?' And I get to be the good guy — I get to say yes."

Ekyndorn Day

Choose a special day to celebrate being a family

"My family celebrates a holiday that isn't on anyone else's calendar: Ekyndorn Day. **Every year on March 20 (the day my husband and I met), we don't go to work, and our kids don't go to school. Instead, we spend the entire day together as a family.** Ekyndorn is our last name spelled backward (well, almost). So far, neither bosses nor teachers have figured this out. The kids love the planning, the secrecy, and the fact that even Mom and Dad 'skip school' for a day."

—Susan Nordyke

WESTCLIFFE, COLORADO

Have a Do Nothing Day

How one family found a way to work downtime into their busy schedules

David Austin of **Portland, Oregon,** realized that his house was filled with activities galore, even on the weekends. And he was determined to find a way to bring downtime back into his family life. Then he thought, "Why not just stay home and do nothing for an entire day?" So he and his wife Maura pitched Do Nothing Day to their kids, six-year-old Julian, and nine-year-old Madeleine. **They would break out of their regular routine and stay home. Each person would pick a fun activity that all four of them could do together. No friends, no distractions, no interruptions.**

The new holiday was a big success. Since then, whenever life has gotten particularly hectic, they've planned Do Nothing Days. David said, "On the corniest, most clichéd level, Do Nothing Days remind us to stop and smell the roses. As a result, our relationships — child to child, and parent to parent — have all been enhanced."

Hometown Tourists

A father and son let the Yellow Pages plan their nights out

"When I began taking a class that met one night a week, my husband decided to use these evenings as a way to acquaint our son, Forrest, four, with our community. He came up with a wonderful exploring method: the Yellow Pages. **Each Tuesday evening, the two of them would open up the phone book and randomly select a business to visit.** Their Tuesday nights took them to such locales as a bakery, a model train shop, an archery range, a violin repair shop, a stable, and a go-cart track, to name just a few. Not only was our son introduced to a variety of new things, but we all came to appreciate the wealth of possibilities in our area."

—Helen Burling
OLYMPIA, WASHINGTON

Neat Twist
SCAVENGER HUNT

To add spice to a stay-at-home vacation, the Seguras of Mesquite, Texas, created a Summer Scavenger Hunt. Everyone in the family added to the list of items, which included a cookie from a local bake shop, a brochure on Hawaii, fishing lures, and the receipt for the smallest purchase. "We had such a great time that we decided to make this hunt an annual event!" says mom Dawn.

Family Adventure Day

Make memories with surprise outings

"About once a month, my husband and I love to surprise our kids with a Family Adventure Day dedicated to fun activities our whole family can enjoy. **We plan our day in advance and don't tell our kids until that morning.** Once we're loaded in the car, the children, Hannah, age twelve, and Dylan, nine, play a round of twenty questions with us. They may ask only yes-or-no questions about what the day holds in store, trying to figure it out before we get there. **We have been to Major League Baseball games, museums, zoos, and state fairs, and have even tried our hands at canoeing and weekend camping trips.** Every time our children hear the words Family Adventure Day, they know the day is going to be a great one."

—Marci Mohan

EDEN PRAIRIE, MINNESOTA

Surprise your kids with a special famIly outIng.

Quick Tip

WATCH THE SUNSET

For a quick and memorable evening, the McDonalds of Florence, Massachusetts, hop in the car and head out to a scenic spot to watch the sun go down, taking along folding chairs, a blanket, a kite or frisbee, and pjs for their two young daughters.

Start a Rotating Diary

A journal helps Mom and daughter communicate

Diane Fowler of Wilmington, North Carolina, shares a journal with her oldest child, eight-year-old Emily. Every day **Emily writes an entry, then Diane pens a response to Emily's message and leaves the journal on Emily's bed. When Emily gets home from school, she writes back before placing the journal on Mom's bedside table.** With three younger siblings in the house, Diane says, "it's hard for Emily to get me all to herself some days. The journal gives her the opportunity to tell and ask me anything. It also makes her feel special and records her individual growth, and it's great writing practice!" Needless to say, the younger kids can hardly wait to begin journals of their own.

Writing back and forth gives a parent and child a private way to share their thoughts.

Neat Twist
E-MAIL EXCHANGE

When Katherine Ambrose, age five, of Portland, Oregon, began reading, her big sister Allison, fourteen, set up an e-mail address for her. Several times a week, Allison sends Katherine stories and messages written at her level. Mom Mary Ellen says Katherine loves to check her e-mail and is proud to be able to read online, just like Allison.

Letters from Afar

On business trips, one Dad sends special deliveries to his two daughters

"Whenever my husband travels on business, he takes along envelopes addressed to our daughters, Kathryn, age six, and Colleen, two. **Before he boards his plane at our local airport, he drops an envelope in the mail to them that contains a letter and small gifts, such as magnets, stickers, or sticks of gum.** Then again at the connecting airport and at his final destination, he puts something in the mail. He continues to send a letter and trinkets daily while he's away. The girls love receiving mail, and these letters make the days he's away easier for them to endure."

When you're on the road, send a letter and a small gift home to the kids.

— **Linda Berkhoudt O'Connor**
ORCHARD PARK, NEW YORK

Share Thoughts in a Talking Chair

Give kids a special place to express themselves

To encourage her children to open up about what's on their minds, **Denise Vega** of **Englewood, Colorado,** designated a comfy armchair in the living room as the Talking Chair. It's a place the kids can head to when they need some alone time with Mom or Dad. **In the Talking Chair, Zachary, age eight, Jesse, six, and Rayanne, three, discuss whatever they want, with "no judging, no reprimands,"** says Denise, "just listening and, if necessary, talking to figure things out." The real key: all conversations are private, "with no one listening in."

Thankful Caterpillar

A paper chain helps one child focus on the positive

"When our son, Joe, turned four, he began dwelling on the 'bad' things that happen to him, such as not being allowed to watch TV whenever he likes. So my wife made a caterpillar head from a piece of paper with markers, googly eyes, and pipe cleaners for antennae, then taped it to the wall in his room. **Each evening, she asks Joe what made him happy that day, such as playing with a friend or going to the park. Wendy writes each good thing on a paper circle, then tapes it up.** Our Thankful Caterpillar spans half of Joe's bedroom, and he has got a whole new outlook on life."

Joe with his very thankful caterpillar.

—Jeff Gerardot
CICERO, INDIANA

Neat Twist
THREE GOOD THINGS

Each day, when her kids come home from school, says Tamara Zurawski of Strongsville, Ohio, they sit down together at the kitchen table with a snack, and she asks them to take turns telling her about three good things that happened that day. "Now they even ask me, 'What are your three things, Mom?' and my day is reviewed along with theirs," says Tamara. "This routine has given all of us a better outlook on our lives."

Workout Routines

Exercising together is more fun for everyone

"I let my kids work out with me, and we make it fun. Although they can't always do what I do (no bench presses for the toddler), **they enjoy doing similar, age-appropriate exercises, such as lifting soup cans and doing knee push-ups.** Even my three-year-old gets into the act: she holds a stopwatch and says, 'Go, Mommy, go!'"

—Shelli Mosteller
CINCINNATI, OHIO

Even young children can find ways to take part in a family workout.

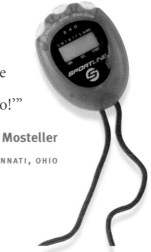

Neat Twist
RACE TRAINING

The Winnetts of Atlanta, Georgia, compete in charity road races together. "Most races have a one-mile fun run, and our five-year-old daughter, Katrina, practices with us between races," says mom Susie. "We are saving all of her race T-shirts, and my mother will eventually make a comfy quilt out of them."

Walking Circle

Get the neighbors in on a nightly stroll

"We have three girls ages six and under. **Every night after supper, we go for a walk around the block. As we go, we add neighborhood families to our walking circle.** Some nights, we have had as many as sixteen people following along!"

— **Bob and Cindy Flaxington**

LINCOLN, RHODE ISLAND

Quick Tip

DITCH THE CAR

In their Guilderland, New York, neighborhood, the Lapinskis are known as the family that goes to the store without a car, says mom Ann. "I walk with the kids' wagon, which gets loaded with groceries. The kids walk, ride a bike, or scooter with me."

Pass the Talking Stick, Please

Maintain order — and lively conversation — with this Native American trick

During one particularly hectic meal at the Schumaker home in Overland Park, Kansas, mom Susan grabbed a plastic flower from a nearby vase and offered her three sons an impromptu lesson in Native American culture. At important meetings, she said, certain tribes enlisted the aid of a talking stick to maintain order. **Only the person holding the stick (or in this case, the flower) could speak. When he or she was through, the stick was passed to the next speaker.** Well, the stick stuck. The boys love the idea and even remind one another not to speak out of turn.

Neat Twist
CONVERSATION STARTER

Around the dinner table in the Doyle house in Springfield, Pennsylvania, everyone takes a turn sharing the best and worst thing about their day. "Many times it's hard to pick from all the best things," says mom Terry. But Terry also values discussions of the worst things. "We all get to share empathy and understanding, and perhaps offer insight into how to handle disappointment," she says. "And we get to hear what's important to our kids."

Candlelight Dinners

Set a calming mealtime mood

Candle flames cast a magic spell at dinnertime.

"One dark winter evening, we discovered a way to bring warmth and closeness to our family dinners. My five-year-old son found a box of half-burned candles, which I had put away because I thought romantic candlelight and small children didn't mix. My son insisted, however, on setting several at the table. **As the family gathered, I lit the candles and dimmed the lights. The flames seemed to cast a magic spell — the kids spoke in hushed voices, and everyone inched closer to the table.** Now, the glow of candles and conversation often fills our house, the warmth lasting long after the flames have been blown out."

— Julie Dunlap
COLUMBIA, MARYLAND

Breakfast for Dinner

The whole family pitches in to serve up a special supper

"On Monday nights, we all prepare dinner together, and we usually prepare breakfast food. **The smallest ones place the biscuits on the pan, and they can set the table if we use disposable plates.** They also fill plastic cups with ice and pass out napkins. **Older kids can peel potatoes and break eggs for scrambled eggs, while we fry bacon and sausage.** Dad cooks the eggs while I pour the drinks and the kids put the butter on the table. This gives the kids something to look forward to because Mondays are so blah. Cooking helps them with math, plus it's just plain fun!"

—Rebecca Bean
MARTINEZ, GEORGIA

Neat Twist
FINGER-FOOD BUFFET

Once a month, the Abelar family of Tracy, California, forgo formality and serve finger food for dinner. Mom Karen sets out an assortment on their kitchen island and the whole family stands around munching. "My two daughters, ages five and two, call this our party night because we don't have to sit at the table and use our forks," says Karen.

Kids Cook Night

A weekly meal where the kids are the chefs

"Each summer when the kids were young, we designated Friday as the children's cooking night. When
Brian was twelve and Dawn, nine, **I began letting them
plan dinner and dessert on alternating weeks. They
chose the menu, shopped, and made or bought dessert.**
Some weeks, we sat down to a candlelight dinner,
and others, we sent out for pizza. I was surprised by
the ideas they came up with and what they could
accomplish in the kitchen."

Designate one
night a week for the
kids to cook.

—Dorris Creter

SARASOTA, FLORIDA

Neat Twist
THE LEFTOVER CAFÉ

When her fridge starts to get full of one- or two-serving leftovers, Sara Prem of Lenexa, Kansas,
turns them into something new with an à la carte menu featuring fun names and descriptions,
such as Refried Refried Beans and Rice, Comeback Cornbread, or Return of the Jell-O, and puts a
copy on her boys' plates. "My four- and six- year-old sons, Dan and Matt, like it when I take their
orders," says Sara, "and they're great tippers, too: I always get a big hug and a kiss."

Spice up the Evening with a History Dinner

Serve meals and movies from another time and place

The Wingfields of Paso Robles, California, mix fun and learning with an occasional History Night. Mom Diane and dad William get most of their dinner ideas from period recipes they've found on the Internet or the Food Network, where **they've learned about foods from biblical times, Colonial Williamsburg, and even ancient Rome. After dinner, the family usually watches a video appropriate to the era.** On Civil War Night, for instance, they ate hoppin' John and hardtack from tin pans and cups, then watched excerpts from Ken Burns's documentary, *The Civil War*. Diane says Kathryn, age eight, and Alec, five, got a real thrill out of seeing characters in the videos using the same kinds of utensils and eating the same foods as they had.

The Wingfields stir up some learning with a Civil War Night.

Neighborhood Dinner Co-op

Cut down on your family cooking time by rotating meals

"Every Monday through Thursday, my family enjoys a delicious home-cooked meal — but I only have to prepare one of them! The secret: four families in our neighborhood created what we call our Dinner Co-op. **The only guidelines are that meals must include at least three dishes (such as meat-veggies-rice or pasta-salad-bread combinations), and they must be delivered between 5:30 and 6:30 in the evening.** We all chipped in to buy a few containers that belong to the co-op so we wouldn't lose our own collections. Because of this great idea, my kitchen stays clean most nights of the week, and I get to enjoy a lot more time with my kids in the late afternoon."

—Marci Johnson
GILBERT, ARIZONA

Create Themed Evenings

A weekly schedule of evening activities cuts back on TV time

To keep the family from just sitting in front of the TV every night, Patrick Schill of Rochester, New York, made up a schedule to follow with Peyton, age eight, and Quinton, five, while Mom is at work. **Monday is Reading Night, Tuesday is Puzzle Night, Wednesday is Games Night, and Thursday is Movie Night. Friday night is Kids' Choice.** Everyone stays flexible, switching a Reading Night for a Puzzle Night, for instance, when the boys want to. And in the summer, Patrick substitutes throwing around a football or going for a bicycle ride for one of their usual activities. "No matter how hard work is," Patrick says, "I always have in the back of my head that I want to get home and do . . . whatever night it is."

Set aside time for the family with a regular Puzzle Night.

Quick Tip

PLAN THE WEEKEND

Every Friday after dinner, the Zobels of Dublin, Ohio, make some popcorn and sit down at the kitchen table with a list of ideas for weekend activities. Options might include strawberry picking, swimming, a local festival, or a picnic. Everybody gets his or her two cents in, they all settle on a plan, and no one is left with that Sunday "Where did the weekend go?" feeling.

Show and Share

On this night, every family member has a chance to shine

"A favorite family tradition is evening Sharing Time, when each child and adult shares a talent, hobby, or something that is special to them. My girls usually share more than one. **They sing, they dance, they share their artwork from school, they share bugs they have caught, flowers they have found.** I still remember my husband coming home with a financial report from work. The girls were so funny with their, 'Wow, Daddy, that's, ummm, a lot of paper. Did you write all those words?' Some nights we have a specific theme for sharing — a favorite song, food, and so on. It's been a good way to get to know and also praise and encourage one another."

During Sharing Time, kids and adults can show off artwork, bugs, and other favorite things.

—Leslie Headrick
AMERICAN CANYON, CALIFORNIA

Neat Twist
FAMILY RADIO HOUR

One night a week, the Fee family of Sagamore Hills, Ohio, create their own radio show. They take turns playing host and interviewing one family member about his or her week or interests. Special features include dramatic stories with sound effects and musical entertainment. The whole show is tape-recorded, so they can enjoy it again in the days that follow.

Host a Family Movie Night

Rented videos and homemade tickets make for an easy evening of fun

Colleen Chavez of **Concord, California,** has created her own in-house Cineplex by posting a "Now Showing" sign with the name of the attraction that will run at the Chavez Family Theater. **The kids use special movie money (sometimes play, sometimes real) to purchase tickets and snacks. "They then proceed down the hall to the 'theater door,' where their tickets are taken by the usher,"** says Colleen. After the movie, the family rates it and hangs the results on the wall.

Neat Twist
MOVIE MASQUERADE

Getonna Cass of Tuscon, Arizona, likes to host Movie Masquerade Nights, in which the kids dress up to match the video. For instance, to watch *The Little Mermaid,* they wore bathing suits and sat on a blue blanket surrounded by water toys.

Drive-in Movie Cars

Transform oversize boxes into personal wheels for a
backyard video viewing

"My daughters, Ana, age seven, and Mary, three,
were invited to their aunt Carol's house for A Night
at the Drive-in. Carol had rented kids' movies,
put a VCR and television on her back deck, and
stocked up on snack foods and mosquito coils. **To
make the experience complete, my kids and I found
boxes big enough to sit in and spent the afternoon turning
them into play cars with windshields, rearview mirrors,
wheels, and license plates.** The cars were such a
hit that their cousins want to have another drive-in
movie night so they can make their own wheels."

—Cindy Gwozdz
TAUNTON, MASSACHUSETTS

Mary and Ana
gear up for A Night
at the Drive-In.

Neat Twist
PARK-IN MOVIE
The Kittles of Jupiter, Florida, haul their VCR and television (or old movie projector and screen)
out to the garage and then climb in the family van for a genuine drive-in experience — with a few
differences. "There are no bugs," says mom Lynette, "and the food is more reasonably priced."

Go on a Nighttime Treasure Walk

A little imagination turns an after-dark stroll into an evening of adventure

The **Abbotts** of **Gardnerville, Nevada,** merged two of their kids' favorite activities — flashlight walks and treasure hunts — to create a new family tradition, Treasure Walk Night. **With flashlights in hand, Aspen, age seven, and Olivia, five, head outside with Mom and Dad to search for sparkly rocks that look like gold, wildflowers, animal tracks, crickets, or anything unusual.** Once, says mom Deanna, "the kids found a bone, probably left by a dog, and were convinced it was a dinosaur bone."

Blackout Nights

Why wait for Mother Nature to turn out the lights when you can do it yourself?

"My family occasionally has what we call a blackout night, when **we pretend that the power has gone out.** The kids — Gina, age ten, Sophie, nine, Logan, six, and Grant, five — run around the house turning off anything that uses electricity: lights, the TV, the stereo, the computer. **We eat dinner by candlelight, then play games, read stories, and color by flashlight.** The kids have a great time, and it's helped them see that losing power can be an adventure, not something to fear. It also provides us with an unusually quiet evening at home."

—**Marilu Hess**
DALLAS, OREGON

Ditch the electricity for an evening that brings the family together.

Neat Twist
BIG BED NIGHT
When Gigi Amateau of Richmond, Virginia, went back to work full time, it seemed her family had no time for one another. So she instituted Big Bed Night. On these Friday nights, they all put on their pjs and climb in bed to eat from a tray and watch a movie. "Big Bed Night is a weekly chance to see tiny moments of tenderness," says Gigi, "moments that are all too easy to miss during our crazy week."

Set up Camp Indoors

Bring the tents and picnic blankets inside for a living-room campout

When the arrival of their second daughter put a crimp in their outdoor camping, the Taits of Danville, California, simply brought the tradition inside. **On family Camp-in Night, they set up a tent and lay out a picnic blanket, sleeping bags, and pillows in front of the fireplace. Supper is typical camping fare, such as hamburgers cooked on the backyard grill and s'mores.** Sometimes they pop popcorn and play a board game. After dinner, they sing songs together and, on good-weather nights, they step outside to stargaze. In the morning, they all share a camp breakfast of pancakes on the griddle.

It never rains on the Tait family campsite.

Neat Twist

FAMILY SLUMBER PARTY

For the Coakwells of Schertz, Texas, Friday-night videos are always followed by a family sleepover, with all five kids snuggled together on the living-room sofa bed. Mom Kathryn gets a kick out of the jumble of snoozing children, ages three to twelve. "Our kids love sleeping together and waking up early to watch Saturday-morning cartoons," she says.

Daylight Savings Party

Celebrate longer days with a sunset picnic

"My family has always looked forward to the change to daylight savings time because it feels like there is more of the day to enjoy together, especially when my husband commuted and would return home in daylight hours. **To make the transition even more fun, my sons, Devon, age five, and Dusty, four, surprised their dad at the train station with party hats, noisemakers, and signs.** We ate a picnic dinner in the park and played until dark. My husband loved it, and we brightened the evening for all the commuters at the station."

— Laura Pierce

VALENCIA, CALIFORNIA

Quick Tip

HOST A STARRY CAMPOUT

The Stouts of Jupiter, Florida, celebrate the annual Perseid meteor shower by inviting neighborhood families to a backyard campout complete with star-shaped cookies sprinkled with sugar "stardust."

Chapter 3

Fun Stuff to Do

Quick games, clever crafts, and creative learning activities to banish the "I'm bored" blues

You know the refrain; it's usually delivered with a dramatic roll of the eyes and a long-suffering sigh: "There's nothing to do." Murphy's Law of parenting holds that you're most likely to hear it when you, yourself, have plenty to do — like make dinner, weed the garden, or pay the bills. The next most common times? During long drives, while waiting in a restaurant for food, and nearly every day of summer vacation. Whether you're trying to keep your clan entertained on a rainy day or just buying a half hour of peace, you'll find this chapter packed with great ideas for jump-starting fun. Flag a few of your favorites and you'll have your kids off and running in no time flat.

Contents

84   Activity Starters

86   Fantasy Play

88   Craft Organizers

92   Mess-Free Painting

94   Recycled Crafts

102   Photo Cutouts

104   Personalized Games

106   Games on the Go

110   Backyard Activities

116   Welcoming Spring

120   Summer Activities

126   Fall Fun

130   Winter Fun

134   Learning Fun

136   Reading & Writing

146   Geography

148   Science

150   Math & Money

Bored Book

A list of options when there's nothing to do

"When my daughter, Jade, age nine, began to complain that she couldn't find anything to do, **I made a list of all of the playthings we have around the house,** including toys, sports equipment, puzzles, and board, electronic, video, card, and computer games. **I added pictures to make it look like a fun vacation brochure, and placed it in a three-ring binder.** We found that because many of the toys and games were tucked away in closets and other such out-of-the-way places, we had forgotten everything that was available to us."

A three-ring binder makes finding activities easy.

—Cindy McNeely
TALLAHASSEE, FLORIDA

Neat Twist
IDEA BOX

Liz Koon of Grinnell, Iowa, keeps her list of boredom busters in a file box. She and her kids (Lindsay, age fourteen, Amy, twelve, and Stephen, seven) scoured magazines for pictures of things they could do (Stephen wasn't reading yet), such as playing with Legos, blocks, clay, or toy cars, or listening to audiobooks, then glued them onto index cards. A quick flip through the box invariably sparks an idea for something fun to do, says Liz.

Project Bags

Simple homemade activity kits give Mom a needed break

"In order to help my five-year-old, Amy, learn to entertain herself when I need time to help her siblings with homework, start dinner, or make phone calls, we invented the Fifteen-Minute Game. **I fill brown paper bags with materials for a short project, seal them, and keep them in a basket for special times.** The important thing is to make the projects simple enough for her to do alone in the allotted time. For example, in one bag I placed pieces of paper with a picture of an object in the house to be counted. Another bag contained the makings of a bird's nest, including yarn, twigs, clay, and candy eggs. I have also filled bags with postcards, pens, and stamps for writing to Grammy or simply enclosed a long-forgotten toy. The game has been a big hit — I get fifteen minutes when I need it, and she gets a new activity to enjoy."

—**Jennifer Caputo**

LAWRENCEVILLE, GEORGIA

Paper bags filled with project supplies make a quick boredom buster.

Quick Tip

JOIN FORCES

Kristine Buys of Orlando, Florida, and her eight-year-old daughter, Katelyn, formed a craft club with a group of Katelyn's friends. Once a week, all the girls go to one member's home for snacks and a craft activity. The Buys hosted the first gathering, at which the crafting crew decorated their own club T-shirts.

Toy Animal Zoo

Create a miniature version of the real thing

"My children, Rachel, age four, and Michael, three, decided it would be fun to open their own zoo. **So we gathered all the toy animals we could find and grouped them according to their species or their habitat (jungle, ocean, and the like).** Then we went in search of containers — everything from a salad spinner to cardboard boxes — to use as holding pens. We had a great time setting up exhibits throughout the living room. Next, we cut tickets out of construction paper and found a stamp to mark the hands of 'tourists.' For about a week, the kids pretended to feed the animals and clean the cages. And anytime someone came over, they 'sold' them a ticket and then showed them around."

Michael gives his Auntie Isabel a private tour.

—Lauren Seeley

BURLINGTON, MASSACHUSETTS

Indoor Safari

Send kids on a hunt for hidden magazine pictures

"Here's a favorite activity for days when my three-year-old daughter, Alicia, and I are stuck in the house. We make binoculars by painting two toilet-paper tubes and tying them together with a pipe cleaner. While they're drying, we look for pictures of animals in magazines and cut them out (if we don't find many, I'll draw a few, too). Next, **Alicia covers her eyes while I tape the pictures around the house. Then she puts on her special safari hat and tries to spot the creatures through her binoculars.** After she finds them all, I hide them again. This activity has given us many afternoons of fun."

Alicia and her homemade binoculars.

—Marguerite Opett
ROCHESTER, NEW YORK

Homemade Craft Kits

These prefab packs make art projects as easy as 1, 2, 3

"I love to buy craft supplies for my kids, Jimmy, age nine, and Amy, six, but the materials often seem to disappear into the closet, never to be seen again. To avoid this, I make a kit that includes the materials right away. I put all the items needed for each project (except things that are always in use, like scissors or glue) in a clear plastic bag. **I then label the bag with a number, the name of the project, and a list of any other necessary tools or supplies.** When the kids want to do a craft, they pick a number, find the corresponding kit, gather the other supplies, and we're all set!"

—Yolanda Pate
HAYWARD, CALIFORNIA

Neat Twist
PROJECT BOXES

When she taught at an art camp, supplies were organized by the project, says Kimberly Stoney of Littleton, Massachusetts. "The brayer, tubes of paint, and special paper went into a box that was labeled 'Printmaking,' she says. "And we had a Paper Marbling box with ink and special paper. Then you never have to say, 'Where are the eyedroppers for this project?' It's all right there."

Craft Supply Station

Stock multidrawer bins with a mix of materials

"I was looking for a unique birthday gift for my daughter's friends and hit upon this idea. **I bought several inexpensive three-drawer plastic organizers at a bed-and-bath store, then stocked each drawer with supplies such as tape, glue, stickers, pipe cleaners, googly eyes, pom-poms, and paper.** The kids — not to mention their parents — have been very excited to get them."

—Jennifer Heck
COLUMBUS, OHIO

Keep supplies like pipe cleaners in easy reach.

A Very Crafty Apron

An old overall bib keeps materials handy

"My six-year-old daughter, Aurora, really likes to make things. To help her keep craft supplies on hand, I designed her an apron from an old pair of overalls. **First, I cut off the overall bib, then I sewed a buttonhole at the end of each of two strips of fabric, which I attached to the buttons on the bib**. To wear it, all she has to do is tie the strips of cloth around her waist. She loves it, and she fills the pockets with her crafting tools."

—**Agnes Lowbrow**
CLERMONT, FLORIDA

Everything she needs is at hand in this art apron.

Marker Cap Keeper

Hold onto pens with this plaster cast

The Levys' marker storage system gets right to the point.

"I have found the perfect way to store my daughters' pens and markers so that the caps will never be lost. First, I filled a shallow plastic container (about eight inches across and one inch deep) with plaster of Paris. **I then placed the caps to my daughters' pens and markers upside down in the wet plaster. When the plaster was dry, we put the pens and markers in their new, permanent homes.** Now the caps don't disappear, and the pens are always ready to use. Mia, age four, and Shayna, three, love it!"

—**Suzanne Levy**
SANTA MARIA, CALIFORNIA

Quick Tip
SHAKE IT UP
Karen Meleen of Lakewood, New York, cut down on mess and waste by filling old salt and pepper shakers with different colors of glitter. Now, she says, her son, Ethan, age four, "can go glitter crazy, and I don't have a big mess to clean up afterward."

Mess-Free Painting

Paint Bottles

Fill bingo bottles with watercolors for fun with less mess

"My daughters, Emily, age seven, and Mandy, four, love to paint with watercolors, but we find the paint cake palettes to be messy and wasteful. **So we fill individual bingo-marking bottles with different colors of liquid watercolor from concentrate.** Each bottle comes with a lid, so you can store the paint right in the bottles, and most importantly, a sponge applicator keeps it from spilling and lets kids control their technique."

Emily shows off a piece of her bingo-bottle art.

—**Lori Ebert**
ORRVILLE, OHIO

Splatter Mat

Protect your table with paper that won't slip-slide away

"When my children, Abi, age five, and Hunter, two, used paint and markers, their art projects always left a big mess on my wood table. Protective coverings like butcher paper, newspaper, and garbage bags just didn't stay put. Then **one day I noticed my leftover Con-Tact paper and decided to stick some to the table in front of each of them.** [Tip: Test first on a small section of the table, to be sure it won't remove the finish.] It stayed in place and peeled off easily — no residue — when it was time to clean up. Now I stock up on it at our local dollar store."

—**Katrina Elliott**
BLACKFOOT, IDAHO

Hunter and Abi are sitting pretty with the help of Con-Tact paper.

Neat Twist
FINGER-PAINTING FUN

To limit the mess when her son, Alec, age four, finger paints, Stacy Cerillo of Levittown, New York, covers her kitchen table with leftover holiday gift wrap, white side up, and tapes down the edges. Alec finger paints on the wrap to his heart's content. When he's done, Stacy pulls it up and cuts sections from it to hang on the refrigerator.

Cardboard Guitars

These homemade instruments get kids rockin'

"Our sons, Alex, age nine, and Ryan, five, love to listen to music, and Alex came up with a great way to make guitars from recyclables so they could pretend to play along. **For each guitar, he attached a wrapping-paper tube to a flat, square box and cut a hole in the center of the box. Next, he taped strings to the top of the tube and ran them down to a taped-on toilet-paper-tube bridge.** The boys have had hours of fun decorating their guitars and lip-synching to music. They have even made some fake speakers and microphone stands to complete the scene."

Alex and Ryan jam with their cardboard-box guitars.

—Jean Hinton

LINCOLN, NEBRASKA

The Fun House

One big box is the foundation for a three-in-one play station

"My three-year-old son, Luke, and I are very excited about the multifaceted play station we made from a large appliance box. **All we used to decorate it was a lot of tempera paint, clear tape, and a craft knife.** We painted one side to resemble the front of a house, complete with a number, front door, and a window with a flower box. Side two became our post office with a stamp window and mail slots labeled 'local' and 'out-of-town.' On the third side we created a puppet theater with a large opening and real curtains. It was so much fun to play in that we even lent it to Luke's day-care class so all the kids could enjoy it."

—Molly Szewczak
COPLAY, PENNSYLVANIA

Luke and his friends can put on a puppet show, get mail, or just play house.

Life-size Portrait

Put together a picture that's a playmate

"One rainy afternoon, my six-year-old daughter, Jordan, and I created a fun activity. **First, I traced Jordan's body onto paper. Then we gave the twin yarn hair, a pom-pom nose, and clothing cut from fabric scraps.** We put makeup and nail polish on her and made her a beaded necklace. We then glued her onto a piece of cardboard. Jordan had a great time, and she loves to show off her twin."

Jordan poses with her self-styled twin.

—Julie Donnelly
GALESBURG, ILLINOIS

Neat Twist
CAN-DO CAN

Gail Costner of Dallas, North Carolina, wanted to help build the self-esteem of the girls in her Girl Scout troop — and teach them about recycling. So she helped them each create a personal "I Can" — an empty potato chip can covered with a collage of all the things they are capable of. The pictures were cut from old magazines and attached using a glue stick.

Dress a Cardboard Clone

Turn a cut-up appliance box, an enlarged photo, and some cast-off clothes into a two-dimensional body double

Inspired by a school assignment that required props, ten-year-old **Dylan Long** of **Chico, California**, and his mom, Regan, made a life-size figure of Dylan's dad, Joe. **First, they traced his body on one side of a cardboard refrigerator box and cut it out. Then, they took a color photo of his face, had it enlarged to life size at a copy shop, and glued it onto the cardboard head.** Finally, they dressed the whole thing in some of Joe's clothes. The finished figure was such a hit, the whole family decided to make alter egos. The Longs' body doubles now spend their days lounging on the front porch, where they've been known to elicit waves from fooled friends.

From left, Nate, Joe, and Dylan look-alikes relax on the front porch.

Colorful Castles

Transform cardboard canisters into royal residences

Abby and a sampling of her whimsical work.

"Like many girls, my daughter, Abby, age seven, loves fairy tales and princesses. So one day she turned some empty oatmeal containers into mini castles. **She covered the canisters with construction paper, added roofs, and decorated the castles with wrapping paper, stickers, popcorn, ribbon, and markers.** She also added tiny flags made from toothpicks and small pieces of paper. Seven castles now grace the ledge in our toy room."

—Jenni Beran
APPLE VALLEY, MINNESOTA

Quick Tip

TUBE PUPPETS
The Ghigliones of Chatou, France, cut facial features such as hair, eyes, and mouths from magazine pictures and glued them onto toilet-paper tubes to make finger puppets. Lucas, age four, and Ben, two, then used their creations to put on shows for weeks, says mom Margaret.

Homemade Paper Dolls

Find figures and clothing in old sewing pattern books

"My daughter, Amanda, age ten, enjoys making her own paper dolls from discontinued pattern books, which usually sell for $1 to $3 at fabric stores. She cuts out the figures, then glues them onto pieces of cardboard. **Amanda also cuts out pictures of clothing from the books, leaving tabs at the edges to help the outfits stay on the dolls.** Not only are these paper dolls inexpensive, but the pattern books offer an extensive variety of people and outfits."

Old sewing patterns gain new life in Amanda's hands.

—Peggy Schulten
ELGIN, ILLINOIS

Neat Twist

MIXED-UP ANIMALS

When his mom suggested he entertain himself by cutting animal pictures out of old magazines for a collage, nine-year-old Jeremy Lobdell of Plymouth, Minnesota, had an inspiration. "He pasted the head from one animal onto the body of another and added the paws of a different critter," says mom Kathy. "We all had a few giggles, and it has become a simple activity he enjoys often."

T-shirt Quilt

Turn outgrown shirts into a comfy quilt of souvenirs

"My son, Jason, age ten, has a number of T-shirts from sports teams he's played on, camps he's gone to, and places we've visited. Jason's aunt, Linda, came up with a creative way to preserve those memories after he has outgrown the shirts. **She cuts a section from the front and back of each shirt, sews them together, and lightly stuffs them to make mini pillows.** She then sews the pillows together to make a soft and comfortable quilt. It's a great keepsake, and as Jason gets older and taller, the quilt just grows with him."

Jason's cozy keepsake quilt suits him to a T.

—**Debbie Emery**

NORTHBORO, MASSACHUSETTS

Stamped Stains

Don't get rid of ruined clothes — redecorate them!

"Rather than throw out my three-year-old son Aidan's shirts when they get permanently stained, I decorate them. **To cover up lighter stains, I usually tie-dye, but for darker stains, I use stamps.** First, I carve potatoes into simple shapes, such as ice-cream cones and leaves. Then I use paint to stamp the shirt with fun designs. It's so easy to do, and Aidan loves to help."

Aiden sports one of his "new" T-shirts.

—**Ann Haran**
OVIEDO, FLORIDA

Neat Twist
FABRIC-PAINTED GLOVES

Sharon Buysse of Marshall, Minnesota, said her four children used to lose their gloves or mix them up with someone else's far too often. So her six-year-old daughter, Tavia, suggested they use fabric paint to personalize their gloves so they wouldn't get mistaken for anyone else's. They all had a blast decorating their gloves. Sharon said, "They are so fond of their creations and haven't lost a pair yet."

Funny Pictures

Make silly scenes by merging photos and drawings

"At the end of school, my teacher gave all the students in my class photos from throughout the year to make our own scrapbooks. With the extra photos, I thought it would be fun to cut out the heads of my classmates to place in funny scenes. **I drew backgrounds like skateboard parks, beaches, and bike trails. Then I taped the heads from the photos onto the bodies I had drawn.** My friends thought the pictures were great. I decided to do the same thing with our leftover family pictures at home. It's really fun to see Great Grandma and Grandpa on skateboards!"

Bryce used extra photos to put friends and family on skateboards.

—Bryce Zinckgraf
FRANKLIN, TENNESSEE

Neat Twist
FAMILY FELT BOARD

Susan Fee of Sagamore Hills, Ohio, turns her not-so-good photos and unused doubles over to her five-year-old, Gabby, who cuts out the people, glues them onto pieces of felt, and puts them on her felt board. Then, says Susan, "She spends hours playing with them and telling stories about her own family."

Mix up the Family Album

Cut and paste old photos to give familiar faces a new look

The Poferls of Champlin, Minnesota, were looking for a new way to use photographs when mom Jennifer hit on the perfect idea. "One of the kids was cutting a picture in half, and I thought, 'Wouldn't it be funny if we could mix up the photos?'"

Over the next week, they shot suitable pictures of themselves and all their cousins, aunts, and uncles. Then they cut the faces apart and mixed up the eyes, mouths, and noses. The resulting album was a smash hit. "The kids loved it. We made one for our family and one for my sister's family, and the kids spend hours playing with them," Jennifer says. "They even make up names for particular combinations, like 'Uncle Chad Funny Bone' and 'Googlyhead.'"

Lucas and Jordynn with a mixed-up family photo.

Make a Chess Set

Mold clay figures to look like family members and pets

Eleven-year-old **Amanda Blue Gotera** of **Cedar Falls, Iowa,** was playing a game of chess with her sisters, Amelia Blue, seven, and Melina Blue, five. It turned out the set was missing a piece, and when their mom suggested they create a replacement from clay, Amanda realized the idea had great gift potential. **Before long, all three sisters were at work on a complete set of chess figures representing each of the Goteras, including baby brother Gabriel and dog Keisha. They used Sculpey clay, which can be baked until it's hard.**

The only family member not in on the girls' project was their dad. His reaction when he opened the set Christmas morning was a moment none of them will forget.

The Gotera family's chess set sports familiar faces.

Classmate Cards

Any way you shuffle them, these custom photo cards are cool

Bryana displays
her winning hand.

"My four-year-old daughter, Bryana, and I made a special deck of cards for her day-care group. Holding a camera so that our pictures would be vertical (like playing cards) rather than horizontal, we snapped a photo of each kid in the class standing against a similar background, then had double prints made. When we got them back, **we glued all of the photos (two of each child) onto construction paper and sealed each 'card' between two pieces of clear Con-Tact paper, trimmed to fit.** The kids have a great time playing matching games, Go Fish, and even Old Maid with them."

—Arlean Azevedo
HILMAR, CALIFORNIA

Neat Twist
FAMILY DICE

Kelly Seim, a teacher in St. Louis, Missouri, used blank dice from an educational-supply store to create a personalized game of chance. With a permanent marker, she wrote each family member's name on one side of each die. On the remaining side, she drew a heart. (You can also use regular dice; just cover the dots with a blank sticker.) To play, the Seims take turns rolling the dice, earning points for the number of hearts thrown.

Customized Car Bingo

I spy a way to speed along road trips

"In preparation for a long car trip, my family created our own bingo game cards. We talked about things we would see along the way, such as churches, cows, ponds, and haystacks. My three kids, Anna, age nine, Eleanor, seven, and Owen, four, drew a picture of each object in a grid of squares. **I made copies of the card, then cut a few apart and rearranged the squares to create three different versions.** We played the game many times during the course of our trip, and it provided hours of fun."

—**Karen Wing**

STATE COLLEGE, PENNSYLVANIA

Annotated Map

Notes and pictures keep kids busy as they ride

"Before my family left our home in Connecticut for a road trip to Florida, I got a fold-up map of the country for my kids and outlined the routes we would take and the names of the cities we would pass though.

On the map, I wrote bits of information about each state (for example: the first gold rush took place in Georgia) and glued on pictures of places in each state. The map kept my kids entertained and busy, but most important, I never once heard, 'Are we there yet?'"

—**Cheryl Sadlier**
DANBURY, CONNECTICUT

A custom map helps kids learn as they follow along.

Neat Twist

MILEAGE MARKERS

Michelle Marek of Rochester, Michigan, came up with a way to make a long car trip pass quickly. On clothespins, she wrote a series of mile measurements, starting with "1,200 miles to go" and continuing with one pin for every 50 miles, right down to a "we made it" pin. She hung a string in her van and attached the pins in order. As she drove, the kids took turns taking the pins off the string, allowing them to keep track of the trip and to see how close they were getting.

Backseat Organizer

A pocket-covered apron solves the clutter quandary

"After a family car trip, my husband and I realized that we needed a way to keep our children's things from scattering all over the car. To solve this problem, I made organizers that could easily hang over the backs of the seats. **I sewed some old pants pockets onto two aprons and used puffy paint to label the pockets for items like pencils, tissues, and books.** I used the apron ties to attach them to the seats. These catchalls keep stuff organized but still accessible, and the kids, Zachary, age nine, and Megan, eight, love them."

This car trip catchall easily ties onto the back of the seat.

—Trish Hazell

ROCKLIN, CALIFORNIA

Make a Treasure Jar

A portable scavenger hunt in a jar offers a new challenge each time you shake it up

Nancy Morrison of **Enfield, Connecticut,** needed a boredom cure-all for a two-hour road trip with her kids, Elizabeth, age nine, and Erik, four. Her brainstorm: create a bottled version of the game I Spy.

First, she gathered a handful of tiny objects from around the house and made a list of all the items. She poured about an inch of birdseed into an empty plastic jar, dropped in three or four of the items, then added some more birdseed, followed by more treasures, and so on, until she was an inch from the top. Then she sealed the jar shut, taped the list to the top, and challenged her kids to find all the objects. A simple shake shifts the order, providing Elizabeth and Erik with an ever-changing challenge.

Birdseed provides the perfect cover for tiny toys and other hidden items.

Play Sticker Tag

In this variation of the popular game, everyone is "It"

The Boudreau family of **Penfield, New York** — Aine, age five, Ethan, two, mom Rebecca, and dad Mark — uses stickers for a simple twist on tag. To get started, **they hand each player a sheet of at least six stickers, then they all scatter to different areas of the yard. On the count of three, players must try to tag one another with a sticker — ideally without getting stuck themselves.**

Your kids will get stuck on this get-moving game.

The Boudreaus don't have any official rules ("We just play until we fall down exhausted and laughing!" says Rebecca), but we thought of a few of our own: 1) You can't tag the same player twice in a row. 2) You can't pull stickers off your own body to put on someone else. 3) You can designate a tree or an area as a base, and so long as you're touching at base, no one can tag you. Once all the players have used up all of their stickers, the person wearing the fewest wins.

The Name Game

Have a ball with this sidewalk challenge

"When I was growing up, my friends and I loved this game, and now I play it with my grandchildren. All you need is a sidewalk or driveway, chalk, and a bouncy ball. Using the chalk, draw a grid with eight squares on the pavement, then write a subject in each square. Popular subjects with my grandchildren include fruits, animals, and cereals.

The first player stands outside of the grid and bounces the ball into one square at a time, announcing something that fits each category as he or she runs to catch the ball before it bounces again. The next child then takes a turn. The trick is that players can't call out anything already named by any preceding player. When someone can't think of anything else to name, he or she is out of the game."

—Carol Fitzgerald
WAYNE, PENNSYLVANIA

Carol's grandchildren love to play the sidewalk game she played as a girl.

The Bike Wash

Make a splash with this squeaky-clean activity

"For my son Carter's birthday party, we had a special activity: a bike wash. First, we built a tunnel from plywood that little bikers could pass through, adding strips of plastic tablecloth to the open ends to make them look like the entrance and exit of a car wash. Then **we attached a sprayer to a garden hose, cut a hole in the top of the bike wash, and inserted the sprayer into the hole so it would rain down on riders passing through.** The partygoers agreed that it was a refreshing way to spend a hot summer day as they lined up along the sidewalk to ride their bikes through Carter's Bike Wash."

Carter comes out clean at his birthday bike wash.

—**Kim Seibert**
LOUISVILLE, KENTUCKY

Make Hopscotch Tiles

Create a permanent game grid with painted patio stones

The **Sheridan family** of **Williamsville, New York,** customized their yard with a personalized hopscotch set. They sanded 10 patio stones, painted them white, and numbered them in order.

From left, Kevin, Courtney, and Michael with three of their stones.

Each child then decorated the stone that matched his or her age, adding handprints and a personal symbol. That meant an Elmo stamp for Kevin, age three, a frog for amphibian-loving Michael, five, and a basketball for nine-year-old Courtney, a serious hoop-shooter. The rest of the stones were adorned with other creative twists. When they were done, they finished each with a coat of clear acrylic sealant, then arranged them in a grid in the yard.

Portable Rice Table

Combine a plastic bin with uncooked rice for low-cost fun

"My two older children, Odelia, age six, and Wyland, four, love to play at the rice table at our local children's museum, so a friend told me how to make one at home for less than $20. **I just bought an under-the-bed storage bin and filled it with a big bag of uncooked rice I got at a wholesale club.** We added some sand toys, and now we have a portable rice table that can be used indoors or out."

Odelia and Wyland share the scoop at their backyard rice table.

—Joann Kiefer
WILLIAMSVILLE, NEW YORK

Neat Twist
ROCK BOX

Cyndie Rauls of Windsor, Wisconsin, created an indoor sandbox by filling the top tray of an old trunk with multicolored aquarium gravel and adding some sandbox toys, plastic containers, clear tubing, and funnels. To prevent spills between play times, she just closes the trunk lid.

Wheelbarrow Sandbox

Make your own moveable play area

"Since we live in a neighborhood with plenty of cats and leaf-shedding trees, I needed a sandbox that would stay safe and clean for my three children, Matthew, age seven, Drew, five, and Isabelle, two. I came up with the perfect solution: a plastic wheelbarrow I found at the hardware store. Filled with sand and toys, it can be rolled in and out of the garage as needed. **Since it's so easy to move, we can set it up wherever we want around the yard — in the sun or the shade — and then wheel it back into the garage at the end of the day.** Our sandbox stays dry on rainy days, and the children can play with it in the garage even when it's snowing out. Plus, when the children outgrow it, I will still have a useful wheelbarrow."

Drew, Isabelle, and Matthew enjoy a day in the sun with their mobile sandbox.

—Clare Collins

WELLESLEY, MASSACHUSETTS

Mini Greenhouses

Fast-food parfait cups get seeds off to a neat start

"Each spring, my kids love starting seeds indoors. To make the process easier, I first collect a few clear parfait or sundae cups from our fast-food restaurant visits. Next, **I buy peat pellets at a local gardening center, and we place one in the bottom of each cup, adding water according to the instructions.** The kids enjoy watching them expand as they soak up the water like a sponge. After the pellets swell, we make a hole in each with a pencil and drop in two or three seeds. We then place the covers on the cups, put them in a sunny window, and add water as needed to keep everything moist."

—Chevelle Kelly
NEW BEDFORD, MASSACHUSETTS

Neat Twist
GRASSROOTS STYLIST

Susan Hellickson of Cedar Rapids, Iowa, satisfied her three-year-old daughter's fascination with cutting hair by filling several pots with grass seed and letting the "hair" grow until it needs a trim. Instead of cutting her own, her dolls', and her brothers' locks, Molly creates grass-pot hairstyles. She also enjoys planting, watering, and caring for her grass, says Susan.

Wading Pool Garden

A plastic pool makes the perfect spot for planting

"Our eight-year-old daughter, Marissa, really wanted a garden. Since we were hesitant to dig up the yard, we instead used a plastic kiddie pool to create a giant container garden. **After cutting drainage holes in the bottom and filling it with dirt, we planted tomatoes, carrots, radishes, lettuce, and cucumbers.** It looked cute and worked perfectly, allowing us to save our lawn. We had a great time as a family watering, weeding, and eating fresh vegetables from it."

Marissa digs her pool garden.

—Barb Ramos
INDIANOLA, IOWA

Flower Hunt

A camera, a matching game, and a homemade reference
book help a mother and son learn about plants

"When my son Brandon was five, he started
to take an interest in flowers and was
constantly asking me the names of plants I
wasn't familiar with. So we decided to learn
them together. With a reference book in hand, we
visited our city's flower gardens. We took pictures of
our favorites and had double prints made. **After playing matching memory games with the photos, we used
them to create our own garden books. We identified each
flower, noting the best conditions for it as well as its
bloom times in our area.** The books came out great, and
we were even able to use this information when it
came time to plan the backyard and borders at our
own house."

You can find all
the information
you need in a flower
field guide.

—Laurie L. Clements

SPOKANE, WASHINGTON

Pressed Flower Hangings

Inspire kids to get to know your garden with a hands-on learning project

"To help our children, Kayla, age nine, Kenny, seven, Kane, four, and Kennedy, one, learn more about the flowers we grow in our perennial gardens, my husband and I came up with this creative learning project. **Together, we pressed flowers from our gardens and then used a glue stick to adhere them to a square piece of muslin. With fabric crayons, the kids wrote each flower's name underneath it and 'From Our Garden' at the top.** We also wrote the season and year in the bottom corner. Finally, we framed the muslin and hung it on our porch wall. We have made one for each growing season — spring, summer, and fall — and my children are now very adept at identifying flowers."

—Kim Scheimreif

WALDOBORO, MAINE

Activity-a-Day Calendar

Lick boredom with this ice-cream planner

"To help fill the long days of summer — and to keep my kids, Evie, age seven, and Gillian, four, from constantly asking 'What are we doing today?' — **I created a summer version of an Advent calendar with an ice-cream cone motif. I cut thirty-one cones from craft foam and thirty-one scoops from felt, hot-glued them together, then glued a felt pocket onto each.** I numbered them, glued the finished cones to two 2-inch-wide ribbons, and hung them up with thumbtacks. Each year, I come up with thirty-one different activities, one per slip of paper, and tuck them into the pockets. The ideas include outings (to the library or the park), activities (baking cookies, throwing a Barbie party), and special events (playing miniature golf). The kids love drawing a slip to see what's on tap for the day. Once we reach thirty-one, we start over."

The Holl sisters with their cool calendar.

—**Shannon Holl**

SANTA ROSA, CALIFORNIA

Enroll at Hogwarts

Liven up summer by giving daily activities a Harry Potter spin

Summer vacation had barely gotten under way when
Pamela Waterman's kids launched into that familiar refrain,
"There's nothing to do." After casting around for a way
to lend the long days some structure and an extra bit of
fun, the Mesa, Arizona, mom hit on the idea of a Hogwarts
Summer Academy. Hilary, age thirteen, Gretchen, ten,
and Brenda, eight, helped brainstorm an impressive lineup
of classes.

They reviewed each week's plans on Mondays in
Divination class. They went swimming during Defense
Against the Dark Currents, played croquet as Quidditch,
fed the fish in their pond for Care of Magical Creatures,
tried out new recipes in Potions class, and opened the
mail for Owl Post. Academy sessions were held each
morning, leaving Pamela the afternoons for her own work.
"Although running Hogwarts involved extra effort on
my part, I enjoyed it as much as the girls did," she says.

Lawn-mower Patterns

Turn your backyard into a tailored play space with a little creative cutting

"Our yard is the main attraction at my family's summer party. To prepare, **my husband first mows the lawn on the highest setting. Then he lowers the blade and cuts a baseball diamond into one side of the lawn and a maze into the other.** The kids have so much fun playing T-ball and chasing each other through the maze. It's an easy, inexpensive way to make our outdoor party a success."

—Nicole Lytle

HINGHAM, MASSACHUSETTS

Ice-cream Tasting Party

Invite your friends to end the summer on a sweet note

"At the end of each summer, my kids and I hold an annual Ice-cream Tasting Party for friends. We buy ten gallons of ice cream, each a different flavor, and line them up on the picnic table outside. The guests stop at the 'registration desk' to collect their flavor-judging forms for rating the ice cream in silly categories such as 'most likely to melt' and 'most

intense flavor.' **Each guest gets a plastic spoon, a small bowl, and a glass of water to clear the palate between**

After the taste test, the guests make sundaes.

tastings. After the tallies are taken and cheers given for the winning flavors, the children make their own sundaes and the games begin, including blind taste tests and whipped-cream fights. This is a wonderful way to end the summer."

—Jennifer Coates

WARWICK, RHODE ISLAND

Quick Tip

PUT THE POOL ON ICE

During the dog days of summer, Julie Miller of Arlington, Texas, freezes baking pans full of water and tosses the ice blocks in her backyard pool. In addition to cooling down the water, they're great entertainment, she says. A favorite activity is "iceberg races," in which players compete to see who can stay on his or her piece of ice the longest.

Beach Golf

Grab a golf ball for a simple, sandy challenge

"While vacationing on the South Carolina coast, we created a game that kept us entertained for hours. **We dug a semicircle, piling up the sides to create a barrier. We then dug holes inside the circle and assigned them point values.** Standing twelve to fifteen feet away, we took turns rolling a golf ball toward the holes. If you got the ball in a hole, you got the designated number of points (we kept score by writing in the sand with our toes); if the ball went over the barrier, we subtracted a point. As the week progressed, we added obstacles such as hills and valleys to make it more challenging."

A few holes in the sand and a small ball keep kids entertained.

—Carrie Russell

GLEN ELLYN, ILLINOIS

Seaside Tea Set

With some plastic cups and a teapot, your child can serve up saltwater "tea" and sand "sugar"

"We took our five-year-old daughter Maddie's plastic tea set to the beach with us. **She happily mixed and served tea to all of us for hours. The sand made great sugar, and there was an ocean of tea available.** And it didn't matter a bit if she spilled while pouring it. We even set up a plastic tub so she could wash the dishes when each party was over."

—**Lynn Grossman**
MECHANICSBURG, PENNSYLVANIA

Neat Twist
TIC-TAC-TOE IN THE SAND
The Heads of Leawood, Kansas, use gray and white stones and a grid scratched in the sand to challenge one another to tic-tac-toe at the beach.

Scarecrow-Making Party

Kick off the season with a few fall guys

"Our family loves autumn, from the day the first leaves change color to the day the last leaves fall. One way we celebrate the season is by getting friends together for a scarecrow-making party. We plan our party for early October when people are starting to think about Halloween. **We send invitations to other families in September, instructing our guests to bring old clothes for their scarecrow to wear. We supply the straw and felt for the faces.** After the last straw is tucked in, we all head inside for a potluck dinner. The next day, scarecrows are perched on front stoops, ready for Halloween."

—Patricia Vara
GAITHERSBURG, MARYLAND

Neat Twist

LEAF PEOPLE

To make raking more fun, the Ayers of Carmel, Indiana, stuff their leaves into garbage bags, prop the bags in the front yard, then add clothing and paper faces to create a faux family. Some years, says mom Brigid, "we've researched a different culture, and dressed our leaf family to represent it."

Autumn Maze

These temporary trails provide hours of entertainment

"My sons, Zachary and Thomas, and I created the hit of the fall season in our neighborhood: **we raked a giant maze of paths (including some tricky ones that were dead ends) into the leaves in our backyard.** The kids on our block had a great time walking through it, and soon they were issuing all sorts of challenges to add to the excitement: racing to see who could get through fastest, who could do it backward, on one foot, while bouncing on a hippety-hop ball, and so on. In the evenings, they went through with flashlights."

Zachary had a ball with his labyrinth.

—Karen A. Solverson
WESTBY, WISCONSIN

Neat Twist
FALL FANTASY HOMES

At their fall harvest party, the Hoyings of Centerville, Ohio, invited each child to design a home, raking leaves into the outlines of rooms and doorways to create a unique floor plan. When they were done, the kids took the grown-ups on a walking tour of their fantasy neighborhood.

Apple Print Shirts

Get decked out to pick a peck of fall favorites

"To celebrate one of our favorite times of the year, my daughters, Heather, age eight, and Kara, ten, and I invited our friends, some local and some from out of town, for an autumn sleepover. **In the evening, we decorated white T-shirts by cutting apples in half, brushing fabric paint on the cut surface, and pressing the fruit on the shirts.** (Some of the kids personalized their T-shirts by taking a bite out of their apples before printing with them!) We accented the apple prints by painting on black seeds, green leaves, and brown stems. The next day, we all wore our new shirts to go apple-picking and visit a cider mill and got many compliments along the way."

—**Karla Paterson**
GRAYLING, MICHIGAN

Pumpkin Snowman

Bridge the seasons by making this simple stacker

"This mixed-holiday project started in my family's garden. **When our pumpkins were ripe, we chose three of increasing sizes and spray-painted them white.** We whittled the stems of the two bottom ones to a point, then stacked up all three nicely. With my help using the glue gun, Timothy, age five, and Sam, three, added a scarf, sticks, buttons, raisins, and the last carrot from our garden to complete their no-melt snowman."

—Christie Youngdale
PASO ROBLES, CALIFORNIA

Timothy and Sam with their harvest snowman.

Neat Twist
TRASH-BAG SNOWMAN

The Masters family of Ellisville, Mississippi, makes a warm-weather snowman by stuffing a double layer of white garbage bags with leaves and pine straw. Stacking three bags atop one another, they use the drawstrings to secure them all to a small tree, then finish them off with pinecone eyes, a carrot nose, and a flowerpot hat.

Snowman Bird Feeder

Decorate a wintry friend with edible treats

"My ten-year-old daughter, Trisha, and I love to be outdoors in the winter and have come up with many variations on the snowman theme. One year, we built a 'snowperson' (as Trisha called it) that doubled as a bird feeder. **We used dates for the eyes, a breadstick for the nose, and raisins for the mouth. For buttons, we slathered pinecones with peanut butter and dipped them in birdseed.** For a belt and trim around the hat, we strung popcorn and cranberries. Last of all, Trisha and I gathered some sturdy sticks for arms, which offered visiting birds a place to perch."

—**Angela Krens**
SUMMERHILL, PENNSYLVANIA

Ice-Globe Lanterns

Illuminate your yard by making cool candleholders

"Following a friend's lead, my five-year-old, Kevin, and I made ice globes to light a path to our front door. **We filled two 12-inch balloons with water, tied off the tops, and placed the balloons outside on a paper plate to freeze.** After three days, we brought the frozen balls inside, and Kevin popped and peeled away the balloons. I ran a hard stream of hot water into the top of each globe to create a hole halfway down the middle. I flipped the globes over and emptied the water and slush from their centers. Then, we repeated this process on the opposite side of the globes to create open cylinders through the centers and put the globes in the freezer. That night, Kevin and I took our ice globes and votive candles outside. I lit the candles and placed our globes over them. Next, we're going to make them with colored water."

—Peggy Shafer

WEARE, NEW HAMPSHIRE

Freeze water balloons to create glowing ice globes.

Snow Day Box

Keep kids busy with a pre-stocked activity kit

"My kids and I keep a Snow Day Box, which is opened only when school is called off because of snow. **It contains hot chocolate, card games, a new unopened movie, microwave popcorn, coloring books, snow-painting ingredients (food coloring and a plant mister), and other fun supplies.** With our Snow Day Box, we look forward to being snowed in for a day."

—**Kim Allan**

CROFTON, MARYLAND

Quick Tip

DESIGNATE TARGETS

To keep her kids from zinging snowballs at one another (which sometimes led to tears), Wendy Hilgenkamp of Arlington, Nebraska, invited them all to stand together and try to hit designated targets, such as trees (five points), snow piles (one point) and the tire swing (ten points). Says Wendy, "the kids all had a great — and safe — time."

Rose-colored Windows

A window "garden" helps end the winter doldrums

"Old Man Winter was hanging around just a little too long for our taste. To help cheer things up and satisfy our longing for flowers, we made our own on the windowpane with washable paints. **Danielle, age six, and David, four, used paintbrushes and their fingers to make the stems, leaves, and different flower blossoms, while Jonathan, two, finger-painted the grass all along the bottom.** Our row of brightly colored flowers was so beautiful that we kept it on the window even after our real flowers had blossomed outside!"

A little paint brought David, Jonathan, and Danielle some early blooms.

—Christine Nowaczyk

MIDLAND, MICHIGAN

Play Activity Bingo

Make learning fun with this twist on the classic game

To keep her thirteen-year-old daughter energized about school, **Sandee Baily** of **Richmond, Virginia,** sets up a bingo board that includes Caitlin's school subjects plus some fun extras and writes an activity into each square. The science category, for example, might include squares asking Caitlin to do an experiment, identify a wildflower, or find an unfamiliar constellation. A fun-and-games category is packed with crafts and games, while the physical-education category requests that Caitlin run a mile, learn how to do a back dive, and so forth. **The Baileys mark completed activities with a sticker, and Caitlin receives a dollar for each bingo.** By the time the board is near completion, a single activity can result in several bingos. And over the year, Caitlin rakes in a veritable educational jackpot.

Stickers mark completed challenges on this bingo board.

Neat Twist

MUSICAL-NOTE BINGO

When her ten-year-old daughter, Kella, started piano lessons, Rebecca Fulcher of Monument, Colorado, helped her learn her notes with a bingo game. She made a grid with the letters "A" through "G" in the various squares. To play, she would point to a note on Rebecca's sheet music. If Rebecca could name the note, she got to mark it on her card with a coin. When she got bingo, she could keep the money.

The Money Tree

Completed assignments count for quarters on this chart

"To inspire my kids, Alex, age ten, and Sofia, twelve, to keep learning during their summer break, I created The Money Tree. First, I painted a tree on each of two pieces of cardboard, one for each child, and hung them on the wall. Each day, I gave the kids several assignments to complete, such as work sheets from study books and reading lessons. **At the end of the day, I taped a quarter to each of their trees for every piece of work they had completed.** By the end of the summer, their trees were full of quarters, and they each made about $12 to $15 to spend however they pleased."

—Teresa Cain

LA MESA, CALIFORNIA

Alex and Sofia cash in on a summer's worth of work.

Alphabet Anglers

Matching stickers make ABCs the catch of the day

"My kids, Jodie, age four, and Nate, three, and I created a fun ABC fishing game using the round metal lids from cardboard frozen-juice cans. **We used pairs of matching stickers and put a different one on each lid. Then I attached string to my kitchen utensils and tied on small magnets.** We have a great time 'fishing' for letters! You can also use color stickers, shapes, or numbers for matching stickers. I plan to use the same idea for spelling words in the future."

Jodie shows off her catch.

—Diana Hornung

OLATHE, KANSAS

Wall Stickers

A changing display offers an easy way to teach kids the alphabet

How do you spell fun? With removable wall-sticker letters!

"Right after my son, Andrew, turned three, he got really interested in the alphabet. To help him learn it, I bought removable wall-sticker letters. **We put up his name first, and some nights before bed we practiced those letters. Within two weeks, he'd learned them with confidence!** So we took those down and put up new letters, which he mastered pretty quickly as well. After that, we moved on to simple words. The stickers peel off and go back on the wall easily, so the letter combinations are just about endless."

—Heather Winn
SPRING CITY, PENNSYLVANIA

Quick Tip
LOOK FOR LETTERS

Virginia Wilson of Columbus, Ohio, and her daughter, Kelsey, age five, challenge themselves to find letters hidden in the world around them. A sidewalk crack might form a K, for example, and a tree branch, a Y. Next, they plan to take photos of their finds and create an alphabet poster.

Sidewalk Chalk Spelling

The best place to study for a test? The patio, of course.

"My nine-year-old daughter, Nikki, got sick of study-
ing for her spelling tests after school, and I wanted
to make it more fun. She loves using sidewalk chalk on
the patio, so I decided to use that activity to help
her study. First, I write each word on a strip of paper
and put them all in a hat. **Without looking,
Nikki picks a word from the hat and hands it
to me, then I read it out loud and she practices
writing it on the patio.**"

Learning is an art
when you write with
sidewalk chalk.

—Cindy Colclazier

CANYON LAKE, CALIFORNIA

Word Pitch Game

A baseball spelling challenge keeps kids on the ball

"I wanted to add a little spice to my classroom's spelling lesson, so I invented the game of Spelling Baseball. **To play, I divide the class into two teams and, instead of pitching balls, I announce words for each child 'at bat' to spell. If the batter spells the word correctly, he or she gets on base,** but if the batter misspells the word, it's an out. More difficult words are worth a double or a triple, and the really difficult words are worth a home run. Sometimes we play outside, and sometimes we set up our classroom like a playing field. This game can be played at home or even at a party, and you don't need many players because you can use imaginary ones to advance through the bases."

—Paul Bratcher

NEW ROCHELLE, NEW YORK

Issue a Word Challenge

Refrigerator magnets help this family feed their vocabulary

At her home in **Portsmouth, Virginia, Dee Martin** takes the whole-family approach to problem solving. When her two preteen daughters were struggling with spelling, Dee gathered up her alphabet magnets and pulled out the dictionary. **On the refrigerator, she spelled out words the family didn't ordinarily use and challenged everyone to incorporate them into their daily conversations.** It worked, and not just for the older kids either. "When our neighbor came over one day and asked our three-year-old how she was doing," says Dee, "she replied that she was morose. I still can see the shocked expression on his face as he went in to repeat the conversation to his wife."

Magnetic letters spell quick learning.

Crack-the-Code Game

Treating letters like a spy code helped this four-year-old learn to read

"When my son, Thomas, was learning to sound out words, he'd often get frustrated and want to give up. To make the process more fun, I adapted a friend's idea for a 'mission impossible' game. I hid small treats, such as jelly beans or all the pieces to a puzzle, in various kitchen cabinets and drawers. Next, I wrote short words on scratch paper and taped them to those 'secret' locations. My son then had to crack the code (sound out each word) to unlock the treasure inside. To my astonishment, he flew through words he'd stumbled over just the day before."

—Amy Burgess
FORT WORTH, TEXAS

Read Aloud Together

Sharing a book gives everyone a quiet break

From about 8:15 to 9:00 P.M. every night — prime TV time — the **Weltons** of **Grove City, Pennsylvania,** gather in their living room, and mom Gaye reads aloud. Meanwhile Andrew, age fourteen, Ben, eleven, and dad Gary each occupy themselves building with Legos, drawing, doing puzzles, or even playing solitaire. As a family, they read about 15 books a year. **"The important things are to choose good books and to be flexible," says Gaye.** For example, if they start a book and find it too tedious, Gaye puts it down and starts a new one. The tradition, she says, has reduced TV time and improved the boys' vocabularies and attention spans.

RECOMMENDED RESOURCES

Good books for family reading, says Gaye Welton, include *For Reading Out Loud* by Margaret Mary Kimmel (out of print, but at libraries), *The Read-Aloud Handbook* by Jim Trelease, *Books Children Love* by Elizabeth L. Wilson, and *Honey for a Child's Heart* by Gladys M. Hunt.

Neat Twist

GOLD MEDAL BOOKS

Taking a cue from the Caldecott Medal and the Newbery Medal, the Hussungs of New Market, Tennessee, have created their own award for favorite works. Steven, age nine, Jonathan, six, and Luke, two, place the Hussung Honor — a silver or gold seal — on the front of any book they feel makes the grade. Mom Rita says the practice has encouraged them to think and talk about what they read.

Mother-Daughter Book Club

Join with other parents and kids for a reading circle

"To help encourage learning, communication, and reading skills among our daughters, my friends and I formed a Mother-Daughter Book Club. **At the meetings, we share some food, talk about the book we've read, and take part in an activity relating to the story.** For example, we made plaster of Paris handprints after reading *The Kissing Hand* by Audrey Penn, and we donated dresses to charity after reading *The Hundred Dresses* by Eleanor Estes. The girls also keep journals in which they record their thoughts about the stories we've read. Everyone enjoys the reading-club format, and the literature and dialogue help the girls develop critical thinking skills."

—Terri Goldenhart

FORT MYERS, FLORIDA

Reading is all in the family for these literary ladies of Fort Myers, Florida.

Reading Tent

A family-room campsite makes books fun

"Getting my kids excited about doing their school reading assignments was not an easy task! But when I remembered how much they love camping, I decided to combine the two. **We set up a small tent in our family room and furnished it with beanbag chairs, oversize pillows, quilts, and flashlights.** When the kids are ready to read, we add a bowl of popcorn or some other favorite snack. The only rule of The Reading Tent is that once you enter, no talking is allowed. The tent has been a success: the kids' reading charts for school are now full."

Turn reading into an adventure with a flashlight and a secret hideaway.

—Linda Hardy
AMERICAN FORK, UTAH

Neat Twist
LATE-NIGHT READING

To encourage her seven-year-old son, Jay, a reluctant reader, to hit the books, Laura Frazier of Stone Mountain, Georgia, picked out a series of chapter books at the library and told Jay he could stay up late to read them in bed. At first, she says, he was just thrilled to be up, but soon he was hooked on characters and plots. The result? A kid whose reading level has jumped — and who can't wait to go to bed.

Trips as Treats

Reward kids for reading with an assortment of outings

"To keep my two sons reading and writing while school was out, **I filled a decorated shoe box with slips of paper, each with the name of a cool destination within an hour's drive from our home.** Some trips were educational, while others were pure fun. After reading a certain number of books (more for my younger son, Danny, age eight, who read shorter books, fewer for Sean, ten, who read longer, chapter books) each got to pick a slip of paper from the box. After every outing, they each wrote a paragraph describing the trip. We pasted photos and the descriptions onto pages, which we put together at the end of the summer to create a 'Summer Reading Adventure' book."

—Sheila Vallancourt
SALISBURY MILLS, NEW YORK

Imaginary Trip

Packing for a pretend journey teaches real lessons about countries around the globe

"When my daughter, Magdalena, was three, we invented The Suitcase Game. We'd put a suitcase on the floor, then Magdalena would toss an inflatable globe and run and put her finger on a country that landed faceup (you could just as easily close your eyes and point to any map, though). Next, **we'd look up the country in a book or two to learn a little about it, then take turns saying, 'I'm going on a trip to ___, and on this trip I'll take a ___.'** From there, it was a giggly race to find what we said we were going to pack and put it in the suitcase. Magdalena just loved this game!"

—Sharon Krasny
NOKESVILLE, VIRGINIA

Quick Tip

TRANSLATE TWISTER

Susan Davis of Sycamore, Illinois, has put the family's Twister game to use helping her kids learn a new language. Instead of using the game's spinner to direct the kids' hands and feet, Susan calls out a color and body part (including everything from toes to noses) in Spanish. Her kids then have to figure out what goes where.

Tabletop Map

Use decoupage to put the world at your kids' fingertips

"Having served us through eleven years of marriage and three children, our kitchen table was in rough shape. It was riddled with scratches, stains, dents, and marker streaks. Getting a new one didn't make sense because the kids were still little, and it would just get ruined, too. Since my two older children love looking at maps and learning the names and locations of places, I decided to decoupage a world map onto the tabletop.

The Soviero kids travel the world without leaving their kitchen table.

I centered a large map on the table and used four coats of decoupage glue to attach it. I let it dry, then covered it with clear, self-adhesive vinyl, available by the yard at a fabric store, to stainproof it. The table looks brand new — and every time we sit down to eat, the whole family learns something new about the world."

—Janice Soviero
MILFORD, CONNECTICUT

Weather Center

A display puts one child in charge of the daily forecast

"When our daughter, Charlotte, was two, we created a simple weather center that she used to announce each day's weather conditions. First, we propped a file folder upside down, like a tent, wrote on it 'Today is,' and drew a large box. We attached a piece of magnetic tape to the center of the box. **We then put words and corresponding pictures that would complete the statement ('sunny' or 'cloudy,' for example) on index cards, and taped a paper clip to the back of each card so it would stick to the magnetic tape.** Before we left the house each morning, Charlotte would look outside and place the appropriate card on her chart."

—Stacey Scheper
BALTIMORE, MARYLAND

Set up a Science Lab

With help from Mom, one kid's closet morphs into a secret workshop

Nine-year-old Bruce Strange has always been a science nut, so while he was out of town visiting his dad one weekend, his mom, Tonya Gordon of Bend, Oregon, transformed his closet into a secret science lab. **She moved his clothes to a drawer under his bed, used chalkboard paint to create a giant computer screen on the wall, and outfitted the room with a desk, clear stackable drawers, battery-operated tap lights, glow-in-the-dark stars, a map of the solar system, and a hook for hanging his white lab coats** (button-down men's shirts from a thrift shop). His grandparents have since contributed a microscope.

Bruce conducts an experiment in his private laboratory.

Make a Measuring Wall

Lengths of yarn and pictures help kids make sense of size

The Watkins family of Rochester, New York, put to the test the theory that kids learn by doing — right on their living-room wall. The project started a few years ago, when Amy measured her son, Derek, then age two. **She tacked a picture of him to the wall at his height, then ran a piece of yarn down the wall to the floor. "Now we measure everything from ants to elephants," she says.** Picnic tables, Big Bird, a bed of tulips — nothing escapes the tape measure Amy carries with her all the time.

Once home, Derek, now five, and his kid sister, Madeline, two, anchor each yarn measurement on a wall with a picture either drawn or cut from a magazine. "Some of our very tall things have had yarn continuing up the wall and onto the ceiling," says Amy. "It's so much fun — my kids are learning measurement, graphing, and comparative thinking without even trying."

Take a tape measure to items large and small.

inch worm
43 inches

Adding Game

A simple card game helps kids practice their math skills

"To help our eight-year-old son with addition, we removed the face cards from a regular deck and played our own variation of the popular game War. **We split the deck between two players, then, on the count of three, each turned over his or her top card. Whoever called out the correct sum first got to keep the cards.** When the whole deck was turned over, the player with the biggest take won. To increase the challenge, we'd play with three people. As our son got older, we subtracted or multiplied the numbers instead."

—Charlotte Meryman

WILLIAMSBURG, MASSACHUSETTS

Quick Tip

PERSONALIZE THE PROBLEMS

Lauren and Howard Lev of East Meadow, New York, edited their daughter's second-grade math book so the problems involve Amanda and her friends and interests. The new version was such a hit that her teacher asked the rest of the kids in the class to do the same and distributed the results as laughaloud homework.

Open a Mom-Mart

A homegrown store helps little earners learn the basics

Tracey Hodapp of **Erie, Pennsylvania**, has found an easy way to make child's play of money lessons for her two young children, Bradley, age six, and Isaac, two, and the other kids she cares for after school. **Every day, the kids earn pennies, nickels, and dimes for completing work sheets and other learning activities. Then, once a week, Tracey opens her Mom-Mart: a big briefcase full of stickers, pencils, candy, and other trinkets that are assigned various prices.** The kids use their earnings to make purchases, so they get lots of practice understanding costs and making change. Reports Tracey, "The children have really impressed me with how quickly they have learned the value of coins and how to calculate what they owe or need to save up."

Book Budget

A personal account keeps spending in check

Kids learn to count their coins with a book-buying allowance.

"Our daughter, Lydia, is an avid reader and is always looking for the next great book to buy through the book clubs at her elementary school. Although these books are offered at discount prices, we usually have to limit how many she can buy. When she entered the fourth grade, **we decided to set a dollar amount that she could spend on books each semester. We set it up much like a checking account, having Lydia keep track of how much she spends each month as well as her remaining balance.** Now Lydia has a better concept of the prices of books, how to prioritize her book lists, and how to live within a budget."

—Mary Sand

SIOUX FALLS, SOUTH DAKOTA

Neat Twist
CHECK REGISTER

Ali, Zach, and Joshua Timm of Park Ridge, Illinois, ages six to eleven, use checks and registers from closed accounts to keep track of their spending. Instead of receiving their allowance as cash, they record it as a deposit. Then, when their mom, Janet, gives them money to make a purchase, they write her a check and record the withdrawal, along with a description of the transaction.

Chapter 4

Raising Kind Kids

Fun ways to encourage good manners, inspire caring and compassion, and keep your children connected to their community

Scan through the pages of this book, and you will see model children: polite, poised, always giving to others. That's because, as you've probably guessed, *FamilyFun* readers have perfect kids. They've never seen a six-year-old clutch his nose and blurt out, "ew, gross" when presented with Grandma's creamed mushrooms at Thanksgiving dinner. They wouldn't know a thing about a sister who hides her brother's beloved teddy bear. And they've never, ever had to bribe a child to write that darned thank-you note to Uncle Elmer. Okay, so maybe they do encounter the occasional teeny lapse in etiquette. But they sincerely wish for polite, happy children, as the many creative ideas in this chapter attest. There are sure to be a few here to inspire your family. Try them — please.

Contents

156 **Manners**

164 **Creative Thank-yous**

170 **Teacher Appreciation**

176 **Friendship**

180 **Family Connections**

188 **Community Service**

Polite by Candlelight

Snuffing out bad behavior at the dinner table

"With three little ones, Kendra, age eight, Gareth, five, and Weston, three, our family's dinner table conversation was always filled with things like, 'Sit down in your chair' and 'Use your fork, not your hands.' To remedy this, **we started lighting six candles at the beginning of dinner. Anytime someone displayed poor manners, we snuffed out a candle.** If any candles were still burning at the end of dinnertime, we all got to have dessert. One wonderful night, all the candles were still lit at the end of the meal, so we went out for ice cream. The kids love the soothing candlelight, and we love the manners they are learning."

—Diane Sitton
SPRING VALLEY, CALIFORNIA

Neat Twist
NO-FEAR DINNERS

The Greens of Castle Rock, Colorado, have helped their four kids, ages five to thirteen, learn to respond graciously to unfamiliar foods by staging occasional "No-fear Dinners," in which they offer up a host of challenging dishes, from pigs' feet to pomegranates. The goal is not so much to eat as to sample with a good attitude. Now, says mom Pam, her kids view new foods as a fun challenge.

Play the Manners Game

When kids act up, they have to ante up

A rowdy group sits around the table, laughing, groaning, and tossing out coins from their piles. Sound familiar? No, it's not a poker game. It's just the Huguet family of Missoula, Montana, playing The Manners Game. **At the beginning of a meal, each player gets a stack of ten pennies, and the goal is to hang onto them — no problem, provided you don't, say, slurp or burp at the table.**

Should you catch another player behaving badly, you must explain to him the appropriate manner before asking for one of his pennies. "My goal was to make it fun," says mom Rhonda. "Sometimes our daughter is laughing so hard, she can barely eat."

Quick Tip

COIN A CATCHPHRASE

What if you were on the moon, and your mouth was full of food, and you opened it? For the Howdyshells of Cuyahoga Falls, Ohio, the catch-phrase "Moon Munch" is the only reminder the kids need to close their mouths while chewing.

This dinner-table game has kids counting their pennies.

Review the Rules

How do you get kids to remember their good manners?
Ask them to say what's right and wrong.

Before the **Stoots** of **Midlothian, Virginia,** go somewhere —
such as the library or a friend's house — the four kids
offer ideas about which manners will be appropriate to that
situation. "Even though some ideas may be unusual,"
says mom Sheri, "all are encouraged." So, **for example, her
kids might call out these rules on the way to the library:
"We don't run" and "We try to be quiet."** What about the
supermarket? "We don't grab." "We don't run into the
pickles!" Everyone remembers the pickle incident (think
pickle juice everywhere). "This way I don't have to nag at
them when we get there," says Sheri. "And I find that
children are more willing to remember their good manners
when the idea is their own."

Neat Twist
MANNERS QUIZ

The Gereckes of the Bronx, New York, have learned to finesse awkward situations through a
Good Manners/Bad Manners Quiz in which mom Sarah spells out a scenario — silly or serious —
and daughters Renata, age nine, and Claudia, seven, fashion a creative response.

The Brother Bank

A shared reward encourages two siblings to get along

"Whenever my husband or I 'catch' one of our boys, Alex, age eight, or Grant, four, doing something nice for the other, such as helping to build a complicated toy, **we reward the behavior by giving him a quarter to put in their joint brother-bank. They can spend the money any way they want, such as on ice cream**

Good behavior is money in the bank for these brothers.

or a movie, so long as they agree on the treat. I've shared this idea with many of my friends, and they all tell me it's helped their kids act more kindly toward one another."

—Joni Gaynor

ANAHEIM HILLS, CALIFORNIA

Quick Tip

USE SIGN LANGUAGE

Sally Ann Hinterer of New Milton, West Virginia, wanted a discreet way to remind her kids of their manners in public. So she taught Levi, age eight, and Dakota, ten, the American Sign Language signs for "please" (rubbing your heart with your right hand) and "thank you" (blowing a kiss). That way she can remind her kids to be polite, politely.

The Good Fairy

Being kind pays off in this household

"When either of my daughters, Natalie, age eight, or Amanda, seven, does something really nice, such as take food to a neighbor or pick up her room without any prompting from me, **I have her write a note to the Good Fairy (a great way to practice letter-writing skills). Then we post it on the refrigerator. The Good Fairy writes an encouraging message back and leaves a small treat,** such as stickers or Gummy Bears, under Natalie's or Amanda's pillow or by her breakfast place mat in the morning. They both love getting the extra praise, and I like reinforcing how important it is to do good deeds."

—Frances Capo
MIAMI, FLORIDA

Neat Twist
SPEED FOR PLEASE
When Philip Langworthy of Reed City, Michigan, was first learning to say "please," his parents reinforced every success by rushing around in an exaggerated way to get him whatever he had requested. The I Speed for Please rule was so hilarious that Philip was extra quick to learn his manners.

Post Kind Comments

An easy way to make family members feel good

At the **Lupreks'** in **Edison, New Jersey,** any compliment or statement of gratitude is jotted down on a strip of paper — "Thank you for reading to me," "I like the way you draw," "You make the best pasta" — and then clipped to the appreciated family member's clothespin. **(Each pin bears its proud owner's photo and is attached to the fridge with a self-adhesive magnet).** "There is nothing like reading what might have gone unsaid between children and adults alike," mom Luci reflects with delight. "The positive energy has increased significantly among all of us — even between me and my husband. Not surprisingly, our lists keep growing."

Appreciation notes get top billing on this family's fridge.

Neat Twist
SPECIAL PLATE

At the Ticknor household in Clarksville, Maryland, a Special Plate encourages family members to say kind things to one another. Whoever has the purple plate at dinner (it rotates daily) is the evening's honoree, and everyone else shares something they appreciate about that person.

Family Awards Night

Celebrate good behavior with pomp and circumstance

"When my girls started the school year with unusually smooth mornings, I was determined not to let their efforts go unnoticed. So, at one Sunday dinner, I announced it was Family Awards Night. **For their good deeds, I presented each of my daughters with a trophy (a can of soda).** Lanie got the Generosity Award for saving her allowance to buy her sister a birthday gift, while Jackie received the Safety Award for helping younger kids board the school bus. My oldest, Leah, won the Self-starter Award for her efficiency at taking 6 A.M. showers. My husband and I decided to make this a Sunday night tradition. Our awards night has boosted the girls' self-esteem, reinforced their good habits, and taught us to look for our kids' positive qualities."

—Patty Kruszewski
RICHMOND, VIRGINIA

Neat Twist
VICTORY CANDLE

When one of their children does a good deed worth commemorating, the Haskinses of Portage, Michigan, place a special candle on the dinner table. The honoree is a secret until supper, when the Victory Candle is lit and the name and kind act announced.

Friday Flowers

Weekly tradition helps one family say thanks

"Once a month, we accept nominations for Friday Flowers: each of our sons (Seth, age eleven, Braden, nine, and Nathaniel, five) — as well as Mom and Dad — has a chance to choose someone he knows and to explain why he wants to thank or honor that person. The following Friday, **we cut three flowers from our garden, or buy them at a local florist or farmers' market, and present one to each of the three people we have chosen.** Friday Flowers has helped our sons to be thoughtful and caring and to look for good in people. Seth, Braden, and Nathaniel have also become quite interested in helping to plan and plant our cutting garden!"

—Janna Mauldin Heiner

POCATELLO, IDAHO

A single flower speaks volumes.

Quick Tip

SHARE YOUR KINDNESSES

Every evening at dinner, the Morrisons of Williamsburg, Massachusetts, discuss a "random act of kindness" each performed that day. These simple gestures may include anything from helping an elderly person in the grocery store to holding a door open for a stroller-pushing parent.

Thank-you Kit

Store stationery, cool pens, and postage stamps in a special box

"To motivate my kids, Madeline, age twelve, and Sawyer, nine, to put pen to paper, I created a Thank-you Kit, **a special box stocked with items just for writing thank-you notes.** Ours contains personalized return address labels, decorative stationery, homemade letterhead (printed from our computer), fun postage stamps (Sawyer likes the reptile and amphibian series), metallic pens, an assortment of postcards, and sheets of stickers. I find they're more willing to write their thank-you notes when it feels like a fun project rather than a boring chore."

—**Charlotte Meryman**

WILLIAMSBURG, MASSACHUSETTS

Fun supplies keep notes from feeling like a chore.

Brainstorm Together

Writing creative thank-you notes is easier when the whole family works together

Ryan Zielinski of **Ballston Lake, New York,** age two, was dictating his birthday thank-you notes to his mom, Dianne, and kept coming up with the same word over and over again. Everything was "cool," recalls Dianne. So **she began suggesting specific things she liked about each gift, "and of course my older son, Justin, five, had to chime in too."** She soon realized they were on to something: it was infinitely easier for the entire family to come up with clever expressions of gratitude than it was for just one of them. They've made thank-you notes a team effort ever since.

Neat Twist
TEMPLATE TICKLERS

To help get rid of writer's block, Kathy Cormier of Palm Harbor, Florida, created a thank-you note template for her kids. Adam, age seven, and Kevin, five, still write out their own cards, but they refer to her sample to get started.

Personalize a Stamp

A simple way to enhance thank-you cards

Turn over a homemade thank-you card from eleven-year-old Nathanial Newman of Bothell, Washington, and you'll see a professional-looking credit: "Created by Nate." His mom, Wren, ordered a personalized rubber stamp to foster enthusiasm and pride. **"It's really made all the difference in the world for him,"** she says. **"Now he's excited to get his thank-yous done so people can see his cards."**

[Tip: To order a text-only stamp — or a reproduction of a piece of your child's artwork — check with your local copy or stationery store, or look in the Yellow Pages under "rubber stamps." Depending on the size and detail involved, you'll pay anywhere from $5 to $25.]

Make your mark with a custom stamp.

Quick Tip

TAKE A PHOTO

For a simple acknowledgement, Beth Van Pelt of Marine on St. Croix, Minnesota, takes a photo of her child holding a home-made "thank you" sign and the gift, and pastes it on the front of a note made from card stock or construction paper.

Day of Thanks

Set aside a special time to show appreciation

"With children ages six, nine, and eleven and a busy schedule, our family never seems to get around to writing thank-you notes for the gifts and favors we receive. Feeling bad about this, I decided to designate a monthly Day of Thanks. **On the last Sunday evening of each month, I sit down with my children, Devon, Ben, and Janelle, to discuss the people in our lives whom we'd like to thank for their kindness.** The first few times I suggested a friend, relative, or teacher to thank, and then we wrote that person a note and enclosed a piece of artwork from one of the kids. The kids quickly began coming up with ideas on their own, and I can see that they really understand expressions of gratitude."

—Shelley Kotulka
WIND GAP, PENNSYLVANIA

A Present for the Postman

Surprise your mail carrier with a thoughtful thank-you

"My family decided to show our postman that we appreciate his work. With a permanent marker, I wrote the following on top of a small tin: 'Postman's Tin: **We appreciate what you do, so we're leaving a treat for you. Take this along and enjoy! Return the tin and we'll fill it again!**' We put it in our mailbox filled with goodies, such as homemade cookies, and we love to see it return empty a few days later so we can plan and leave our next surprise."

—Anita Terpstra
VALLEY CENTER, KANSAS

Way to Go, Coach!

Have a ball making this clever thank-you gift

"Here's the unique present my kids, Kori, age eight, and Colton, twelve, and I came up with for their soccer coaches at the end of the season. About eight weeks ahead of time, we planted grass seeds in large plastic cups. [Tip: You can transplant a little from the edge of your yard if you don't have time to grow it from seed.] Next, we made large sugar cookies and baked them with wooden skewers inserted like lollipop sticks. **We frosted half of the batch of cookies to look like soccer balls; on the other half we wrote 'Thanks, Coach!' with icing.** We stuck one of each in each cup so the cookies looked like balls resting on the grass and attached a note that read 'Thanks for a sweet season.' The coaches loved them."

Coaches will get a kick out of this end-of-season gift.

— Michelle Thompson
SMITHFIELD, UTAH

Handprint T-shirt

Names and prints make the grade in this project

"My daughter Chloe's preschool class made these T-shirts as an end-of-the-year present for their teachers. **With fabric paint, all of the kids put a handprint on the back of each shirt.** (I slipped heavy paper inside the shirts so the paint wouldn't bleed through.) With a fabric-paint pen, **I then wrote every student's name underneath his or her print.** On the fronts of the shirts, I used foam letter stamps to spell out 'This preschool teacher deserves a pat on the back!'"

—**Amy Dennis**

SWANZEY, NEW HAMPSHIRE

A class effort makes a handy gift for a teacher.

A Collection of Compliments

When it comes to thanking your teacher, one T says it all

"My son, Jacob, age nine, had a wonderful teacher named Miss Lizik. As the school year came to a close, I wanted to help the kids do something special for her. First, **I sent home a note with the children asking each of them to finish the sentence 'What I like best about you, Miss Lizik, is . . .'** Meanwhile, I bought a T-shirt at the local print shop and had the phrase 'What we like best about you . . .' printed on the front of it. Then I used a fabric marker to copy each response onto the T-shirt, with each child's name under his or her quote. Miss Lizik loved it."

—Linda Chilko Slater

ALLEGHENY TOWNSHIP, PENNSYLVANIA

Neat Twist

SELF-PORTRAIT T-SHIRT

To create a memorable teacher gift, Julie Walton of New Providence, Pennsylvania, and other parents at her son's preschool had each child in the class draw a colorful self-portrait and sign their name on a 4- by 6-inch piece of paper. The drawings were then scanned into a computer, printed onto iron-on transfer paper, trimmed, and ironed all over the front and back of a white cotton T-shirt, along with the message "Thanks for a great year, Mrs. Davey."

Terrific Tote

A homemade gift lets kids give their teacher a thumbs-up

"My daughter Meghan's preschool teacher was retiring, and I thought that a personalized tote bag would make a great gift. **I had all the students use fabric paint to put their thumbprints on a canvas bag, then sign their names underneath their prints with a fabric pen.** After the paint dried, I made each thumbprint look like a child, adding arms and legs and other details, and wrote at the top 'You are thumbody special.' The bag made a nice, functional keepsake for their teacher, and the kids and I had a lot of fun making it."

—Jen Mock
JOHNSTOWN, PENNSYLVANIA

A tote bag with thumbprint kids lets a teacher know she is "thumbody" special.

Neat Twist
HEARTFELT BAG

Emma Cummings-Krueger of Minneapolis wanted to give her first-grade teacher, Ms. Jansen, a gift from her heart, so she covered her palms in fabric paint, then pressed her hands, overlapping, onto the front of a tote bag to form a heart shape. Next, Emma and her mom, Megan, wrote across it, "Thanks for the warm hugs and warm heart."

Give a Gift Certificate

Thank a teacher for her efforts with redeemable coupons

Since teachers aren't the highest paid professionals in the world, **a gift certificate — to a bookstore, a restaurant, or even a school-supply outlet — is sure to be deeply appreciated.** Here are a few suggestions:

Debbie Ellenz of Camas, Washington, helped her daughter, Katie, make a card for her teacher that read "Thanks a latte!" and presented it to her with a gift certificate to a local coffeehouse.

Teacher Sharon Golden of Conyers, Georgia, says the best present a student ever gave her was a gift certificate to a local spa. The attached note said, "You work so hard doing everything for others. It's time that you do something for yourself. Enjoy!"

The gift that keeps on giving.

Assemble a Reading Basket for the Classroom

Give a group gift to a special teacher

Second-grade teacher Jamie Ball was a true inspiration to her student **Eben Zboch** of **Charlotte, North Carolina.** "She just took him under her wing," says Eben's mom, Rhonda. "She took them all under her wing. She really went out of her way to find what was special in every child." Miss Ball also improved the kids' reading skills that year, so as a fitting thank-you, Rhonda coordinated a class gift. **Each student donated a copy of his or her favorite book, and Rhonda placed them all in a wicker laundry basket.** "Miss Ball was so touched," says Rhonda, who described how the teacher kept the basket beside her reading chair. "She now has books for her class, a basket to store them in, and a gift from the students' hearts."

A collection of student favorites is sure to please.

Summer Survival Kit

A fun pack starts a teacher's break off right

"When my son, Kevin, was finishing up kindergarten, he wanted to do something special for his teacher. We came up with the idea of giving her a present that would help her enjoy her summer vacation. **We bought a brightly colored tote bag and filled it with such items as sunscreen, funny sunglasses, inflatable beach balls, and a novel.** My son then made a large sun out of paper and decorated it with crayons and glitter. I wrote 'My Teacher's Summer Survival Kit' on it and we taped it to the bag. We've been giving these kits ever since, and all of his teachers have loved them."

—Wanda Nelson

SAN DIEGO, CALIFORNIA

Pen-pals Kit

An end-of-school gift helps separated friends stay in touch

"My son, Joey, became upset at the end of preschool. He had made a lot of friends, and he knew he would not be seeing them as often in the summer — or in his new kindergarten class. After many tears and some brainstorming, we came up with the **Friendship Package: an envelope containing a cool pen, postage stamps, and homemade postcards preprinted with our address.** We even included fill-in-the-blank sentences (such as 'My favorite part of summer was ___.') on the postcards to make it easier for both the kids and parents. The children were able to keep in touch with each other over the summer, and they learned a little bit about being a great pen pal."

—**Kimberly R. Kanoza**
PITTSBURGH, PENNSYLVANIA

Neat Twist
CALLING CARDS

The Hestleys of Solon, Ohio, know a thing or two about making and keeping friends, having moved seven times in eight years. On their home computer, they designed business cards with each kid's name, new address, phone number, e-mail address, and photo. Gretchen, age nine, and Nathan, eleven, pass the cards out to old classmates when they leave and to new ones when they arrive.

Get-to-Know-You Guest Book

As a visitor to this house, you'll have to answer a few questions

"We've found a great way to learn more about our friends and family. **Each visitor to our home fills out a sheet that includes ten or so questions, such as 'My favorite foods are ___' and 'My hobbies are ___.'** We keep the question sheets in a three-ring binder on our coffee table. When our kids' friends come over, they rush to the binder to read the latest entries."

—Julie Shiroma
DIAMOND BAR, CALIFORNIA

Quick Tip

CREATE A KIDS' PHONE BOOK

To make it easier for her six-year-old daughter to call friends and relatives by herself, Anne Robinson of Cuyahoga Falls, Ohio, glued a photo of each person onto a sheet of paper, along with the name and phone number, and placed them all in a three-ring binder.

A Shared Scrapbook

Helping two friends stay connected after a move

"When our family relocated, my six-year-old daughter, Jenna, and her best friend, Paige, were sad about being separated. To help them keep in touch, Paige's mom bought a blank scrapbook and sent it to our new home after we arrived. **She included instructions that Jenna was to fill one page with such things as a letter, photos, and mementos, and then mail it to Paige, who would do the same.** They sent it back and forth for a year before it was complete, and then I made a color copy for each of them. I love this idea because my daughter learned that a special friend can always be a part of her life, even when she's far away."

—Susan McClane
RIDGEFIELD, CONNECTICUT

Long-distance pals Paige, left, and Jenna.

Neat Twist
FRIENDLY GIFT WRAP

Angie Foster-Goodrich of Kalamazoo, Michigan, and her daughter created personalized wrapping paper for a present to Kelsey's friend by making multiple photocopies of a photo of the two girls together, then painting the pictures crazy colors.

Framed Farewell

Say good-bye with a personalized keepsake to
hang on the wall

"When our well-loved neighbors were

getting ready to move away, the rest of the

neighborhood wanted to send them off with some-

thing special to show we'd miss them. **I purchased**

a picture frame and mat with multiple openings at a craft

store, and each family was responsible for filling two

openings, one with a snapshot of their family and one

with a good-bye message. Before our friends left,

we presented them with the keepsake so they would

remember our wonderful neighborhood."

Luke and his
neighbors made
this good-bye gift
for their friends.

— Molly Szewczak

WHITEHALL, PENNSYLVANIA

Send Kids' Artwork

Keep in touch with care packages bearing notes and artwork

In this age of family Web sites, chat sessions, e-mail, and conference calls, good old-fashioned snail mail can still play an important role in keeping families close. For the **Petrie family** of **Bernardsville, New Jersey,** it's a brilliant vehicle for recycling five-year-old Madigan's and two-year-old Maren's artwork. "Our girls produce more paintings, drawings, and collages than we ever could save," says mom Darcy. "So, **when the art room is full, we gather the extras, add notes or Post-its to the backs, and send them off.** Great-Gram can always use another scribbled purple cat, and those few sentences help us stay in touch when we don't have time for a proper letter."

Neat Twist
PHOTO MAILERS

The Enrights of Lombard, Illinois, have found an easy way to stay in touch using extra photos. They just write the recipient's address and a brief message on the back of a photo, cover the front with clear Con-Tact paper, and drop the card in the mail with a postcard stamp.

Birthday of the Month

Celebrate far-flung relatives' birthdays — even when they can't attend

"We don't live close to grandparents, aunts, uncles, or cousins, but my husband and I still want them to be a big part of our children's lives. **To help maintain close relationships, we throw a birthday party once a month for a faraway family member.** We do things like sing 'Happy Birthday,' eat a treat, tell stories about that person, and give him or her a call. This tradition allows my kids to learn more about our loved ones, feel involved in their lives, and, of course, have a lot of fun."

Rachel, age four, stands in for the guest of honor.

—Leslie Albrecht Huber

MADISON, WISCONSIN

Neat Twist

HONOR A FAMILY MEMBER NIGHT

The Rivases of Portland, Oregon, occasionally devote a night to honoring a distant relative. The three kids, ages two to eleven, interview the honoree over the phone ahead of time about his or her favorite foods, colors, and so on, then use the answers to plan a special dinner.

Chain Mail

An extended family stays close with revolving letters

"My family is scattered throughout the United States, which makes phone calls expensive. We came up with a good way to stay in touch that's fun and not time-consuming. We call it 'Myers Mail.' **I'll write a letter and send it to my sister. Once she's read it, she adds a letter of her own and pops them both in the mail to my brother, who then adds his family's letter to the batch, and so on until the whole family has participated.** The last person in the chain sends them all back to me. I remove my original letter, add a new one, and send the whole pack to my sister again, who does the same. I eagerly look forward to finding these personal letters from my family in the mailbox."

—Mary (Myers) Groves

TROY, OHIO

Pass the news around with a traveling package.

Neat Twist

CUSTOMIZED CLIPPINGS

In Vancouver, British Columbia, the Allison family keeps in touch by mailing out newspaper clippings. Every day, Cathy Allison and five-year-old Emma peruse the paper, cutting out articles and comics that appeal to the interests of various family members (dogs for Aunt Leanne, rock bands for Uncle Bill, and so on). At month's end, Cathy and Emma enclose the clippings with a family newsletter.

Monthly Mailings

Membership in a made-up club helps relatives
stay in touch

"My sister, Katie, was determined to stay in close
contact with my kids even though she lives in Texas.
Her clever idea accomplished that and took care of her
Christmas presents at the same time! **She picked one
theme per child, then gave each a "membership" to a made-
up monthly club:** a horse-of-the-month club (through
which she promised a plastic pony, for instance, or
horse stickers) for Emma, age five; a lollipop-of-the-
month club for Ian, seven; and a surprise-of-the-month
club (hair bands or rubber stamps) for Elizabeth, ten.
Every four weeks, the kids all put one of the vouchers
Aunt Katie gave them (plus letters and photos) into
a preaddressed, stamped envelope (also supplied by
Katie). Soon after, a small package arrives with a letter
and the promised goodies."

— Jennifer Harris
SACRAMENTO, CALIFORNIA

Familiar Faces

Keep distant relatives in mind with a game of concentration

"While brainstorming for a one-of-a-kind gift for my kids, **I came up with the idea of using photos of family members to make a homemade version of the matching game Memory.** I started with a bunch of snapshots, and made duplicates or color copies so I had two of each image to use. Then I trimmed them, mounted them on uniform pieces of card stock, and laminated them (Con-Tact paper would work, too). In addition to being fun to play, this game is a great way for my kids to familiarize themselves with relatives they don't see often — and we all get to reminisce over pictures of ourselves at parties and on vacation."

—Lori Goldsmith
WEST JORDAN, UTAH

Neat Twist
BLOCK HEADS
Pamela Greer of Ramona, California, made customized blocks for her grandson using photos of everyone in his family, including aunts, uncles, cousins, grandparents, and his mom and dad. She first painted the blocks bright colors, then decoupaged a photo onto each side.

Cousin Collage

Post a family photo gallery on the fridge

"Since our large extended family gets together only about twice a year, my kids go for long periods without seeing their cousins. At one recent gathering, I noticed that it took the kids a while to warm up and become comfortable with one another after so many months apart. **To help my kids feel close to their cousins, we created a 'cousin collage' and posted it on the refrigerator.** We take new pictures of the kids at each family get-together and add them to the collage so they can be reminded of the fun they had together and look forward to the next visit."

—Jane Dutra-Salemi
CAMINO, CALIFORNIA

Neat Twist
BABY FACES

For a fun, kid-friendly twist on the traditional family tree, Melissa France of Flemington, New Jersey, solicited baby pictures from all her kids' relatives — from grandparents to newborn cousins — then framed the photos and displayed them together.

Photo Stories

Capture family history with old photographs and a cassette recorder

"When my grandfather, Hal, was in his eighties, my father arranged a storytelling session with him, using photos from Hal's ranching days in Montana in the 1920s and 1930s. **Dad brought a stack of family photos, each numbered on the back. After the number was read onto the cassette tape, Hal described the people and places in the photo and spun out colorful tales** of ranch hands, wolf encounters, rodeos, and life on the range. The result is a priceless set of cowboy stories that our family will enjoy for generations to come."

—**Rani Arbo**
MIDDLETOWN, CONNECTICUT

Quick Tip

MAKE A GAME OF PAPA'S LIFE

Using a piece of cardboard covered with white cloth, thirteen-year-old Bailey Bell of Leavenworth, Kansas, created a board game of her grandfather's life. Squares contained instructions related to his favorite activities, and the whole thing was packed in a decorated pizza box, along with dice, playing pieces, and directions.

Door Decor

This art project helps generations connect

"When my kids' great-grandmother moved into an assisted-living home, **my children and I came up with the notion of decorating her door every month with a seasonal theme.** It gives Mary Jane, age seven, and Mark, six, something to do when we see her and a new place to display some of the beautiful artwork they've made that month. It also helps ensure timely visits on our part. The kids put a lot of thought into planning Grandma's door (we regularly collect contributions from the sixteen other great-grandchildren), and they now really look forward to seeing her. Plus, Grandma has been getting lots of attention from people who stop at her door to admire the kids' efforts."

—Amy Voss
OSWEGO, ILLINOIS

Mark and Mary Jane, with their great-grandmother, proudly display their door decoration.

Neat Twist
WALL-TO-WALL VISITORS
The Leonhard kids of Raleigh, North Carolina, created paper versions of themselves to keep their grandmother company during an extended hospital stay. They dressed their look-alikes in patterned wrapping paper and construction-paper shoes, added curling ribbon hair, and hung them up.

Nursing-home Angel

Child sees the difference his volunteering makes

"My thirteen-year-old son, Jeremy, and I regularly go to a local nursing home, where we volunteer on the floor that has residents with dementia and mild Alzheimer's. **Jeremy loves getting the patients drinks, pushing their wheelchairs, and playing catch.** One of his most memorable experiences was with a resident who couldn't speak. She was crying, so he hugged her and told her it was okay. He asked her what her name was, repeating the question a few times. She finally looked up at him and said her name, then added, 'Oh, I love you,' and kissed his hand. Ever since that moment, she has been smiling and talking a little bit. It amazed our family, as well as the nursing-home staff and some of the residents. See how a small gesture can affect someone's life? As he continues to volunteer, the residents tell him he is their angel."

—Kathleen Bentham

WEST CHICAGO, ILLINOIS

Make Crafts with the Elderly

Host a monthly activity class at a retirement community

Lori Richardson of **Indianapolis** and her daughter Rachel, age eight, turned their passion for crafts into a volunteer project at the nearby Forest Creek Commons retirement community. About 15 residents attend their monthly Heavenly Crafts class. **Lori and Rachel pick out a simple craft and buy supplies in advance, then Rachel demonstrates how to make it.** Her favorite so far: flag pins out of Shrinky Dinks for the Fourth of July. Rachel enjoys it so much, she plans to continue. "When I'm older, I'll be just like my mom. I'll teach people how to do the crafts, and my little girl will help me out," she says.

Share your skills with simple craft projects.

Neat Twist
CRAFT BAGS

To help entertain patients at Children's Hospital in Philadelphia, where her three-year-old brother was treated for asthma, Adrienne Alexis, age ten, of Browns Mills, New Jersey, and her mom, Ninotchka Ruiz, filled more than 60 gift bags with arts-and-crafts supplies. Materials were donated by family and friends or bought with money Adrienne raised through a yard and bake sale.

Deliver Meals on Wheels

Kids join their mom in a family effort

Even very young children can volunteer. Just ask Jodi
Graham Wood of Sioux City, Iowa, who has been delivering
Meals on Wheels with Anna, age three, and Stephen, two,
since Stephen was an infant. **Once a week, Jodi picks up
prepared meals at a hospital, then drives to an apartment
building, where the trio bring meals to about 10
households.** Stephen goes in the stroller, hot
meals go in the thermal bag over Jodi's shoulder,
and cold items go in a basket over her arm. Anna
leads the way. Anna hands over the cold items,
while Mom dispenses hot things. The whole
activity takes about an hour. "It makes Anna
happy to give food to people," says Jodi. "She
asks, 'Do we do Meals on Wheels today?' and she's excited
when the answer is yes."

The Woods' family
project feeds
body and soul.

Little Brother for the Day

Become a Big Family through the Big Brothers Big Sisters program

"Our family consists of my husband, myself, and our eighteen-month-old son. We spend time weekly with a 'little brother' we were matched with through our local Big Brothers Big Sisters program. **We do fun stuff as a family, and our son loves getting to have a 'brother' for the day.** We go swimming and to movies, or just hang out at our house and bake cookies. A lot of people don't know about the option to become a Big Couple or a Big Family — it is a wonderful experience."

—Maggie Modjeski
WINONA, MINNESOTA

Collect Sneakers for Kids

A gym-shoe drive turns into a long-term community project

When **Brita Thomas** of **Moorhead, Minnesota,** was in fourth grade, she noticed a classmate who always sat out of gym class. One day, she asked why. The girl confided that her parents couldn't afford to buy her sneakers, and kids weren't allowed to play without them. **When Brita went home that day, she asked her mom, Noreen, if she could spend her allowance to buy shoes for her classmate. Noreen got an okay from the principal, and in the process she learned of more kids in need.** Brita's family (Noreen, dad Lee, Evan, age twelve, and Carsten, ten) realized they couldn't solve the problem by themselves, so they enlisted the help of the kids' 4-H Club. The result was Happy Feet, a group started with a first-year goal of giving away 250 pairs of sneakers. Thousands of volunteer hours and pairs of shoes later, they have exceeded their wildest dreams.

The Thomases help other kids get the footwear they need.

Ice-cream Drive

One family turns frozen treats into help for the hungry

"My children and I enjoy turning our van into an ice-cream truck, an idea my twin nine-year-old daughters, Whitney and Haley, came up with. We decorate our van with drawings of ice-cream cones and such, load up a cooler with frozen treats, and head out to the homes of our friends and neighbors. A few phone calls ahead of time and a cowbell (rung by my son Hall, age six) help announce our arrival. **The twist to the Ballinger Family Ice Cream Truck, however, is that rather than take money for the frozen treats, we instead collect canned goods from our patrons. The following day, we drive down to the food bank to deliver the supplies we've gathered.** Not only is it a fun way to spend a sunny summer day, but we get to help others as well."

—Tawni Ballinger

GERMANTOWN, TENNESSEE

Quick Tip

HOLD A SEWING PARTY

The Schleiers of Phoenix, Arizona, helped other families on their street sew pillowcases for kids in a local shelter. At the day-long work party, each of the 25 children and five adults was given an important job, from pinning hems to running a sewing machine. The group made more than 100 pillowcases and matching drawstring bags for toiletries or other small belongings.

Decorate School Walls with Handprint Tiles

Turn an art project into a big-ticket fund-raiser

When the elementary school on **Anna Maria Island** in **Florida** needed money for a new playground, its fund-raisers thought big. They turned a $35,000 profit in less than a year by selling decorative tiles that kids and local businesses could personalize and hang on the walls of the school. **"Each child in the school got to put her name and handprint on a tile, and we asked parents to pay $25 for it,"** says fund-raiser mom **Lynn Lott.** The 6- by 6-inch tiles cost the organizers $5 each, and orders were paid for in advance, so little capital was needed. A set of tiles for businesses went for $100, and some generous area businesses bought big. No child was excluded, Lynn explained — kids whose parents opted not to buy a tile still got to add one to the wall. "The kids are always showing off their tiles," says Lynn. "They take so much pride in it."

Quick Tip

DELIVER THANKS WITH ORDERS

Lynn Grossman of Mechanicsburg, Pennsylvania, says that when her daughter, Megan, sells candy and wrapping paper for school fund-raisers, she thanks her customers for their support by attaching a note to each order she delivers.

Parties for Charity

One family remembers those in need when planning a party

"Whenever our family hosts a birthday or holiday bash for the kids, **the invitation always includes a request for specific donations. One Christmas, we asked each family to bring a pair of mittens, then donated them to a school to give to kids in need.** At my daughter's birthday party, we asked the kids to bring backpacks,

which we donated to a local foster children's organization. My children enjoy brainstorming an appropriate gift for each event, and it teaches them the importance of charity."

The kids decide together what item to collect.

—**Beth Vona**

CICERO, NEW YORK

Quick Tip

CREATE A CARING CAN

To encourage her daughter's philanthropy, Leslie Garisto Pfaff of Nutley, New Jersey, doubled her daughter's allowance and had her put half of the increase in a savings account and the other half in a Caring Can, for giving to charity. Lily, age eight, researches causes and decides on her own where to donate the money.

Chapter 5

Milestones & Memories

Simple ways your family can mark meaningful moments and create special keepsakes

Ask your child what she remembers about a trip to the beach and you're likely to hear about the little things: the speckled pebble she found in the surf, or how the wind took Daddy's hat away. That's because, as any kid can tell you, the delight is in the details. Creating special memories doesn't take lots of time or money, just a willingness to pay attention to the moments as they sail by. The big milestones, like birthdays, new school years, and the arrival of a sibling, offer plenty of fodder for the family album. But so do the little ones: the skills mastered, heights reached, and passions pursued. On the pages that follow, you'll find our readers' favorite tips for honoring and preserving a range of kid occasions, all designed to help you enjoy each one to the fullest.

Contents

198 Birthday Traditions

206 Welcoming a New Baby

208 First Day of School

214 Family Keepsakes

218 Vacation Memories

Festive Wake Up

Greet the day with a display of birthday messages

"After our birthday child is in bed, my husband and I blow up balloons and make mini-posters wishing her a happy birthday. **When she wakes up the next morning, she is greeted with a big bunch of balloons hanging on her door, and she finds more balloons and posters on her way to the kitchen.** As the kids have gotten older (they are ages twelve, nine, five, and two), they help get posters and balloons ready for the younger ones. One year, even I woke up to balloons. My two older girls waited patiently in bed for me to go to sleep so they could surprise me. 'It's tradition, Mom,' they said."

—**Toni Moll**
CAPE GIRARDEAU, MISSOURI

Quick Tip

BIRTHDAY FAIRY

Each year, the Birthday Fairy visits the Smithhisler twins of Indianapolis, Indiana, while they're sleeping. On their birthday morning, they wake to presents left at their places at the dining room table.

Breakfast Treat

Rolls arranged into a number shape honor the birthday child

"Our family loves to celebrate each other's birthdays. To get the day off to a good start, **we like to make a special breakfast: cinnamon rolls arranged on a large cookie sheet or platter to form the birthday boy's or girl's age** (we use refrigerated rolls, so it's always quick and easy to make). We even put a candle in one of the cinnamon rolls and sing 'Happy Birthday' before he or she blows it out!"

Jean's daughter Jackson and her seventh-birthday breakfast.

—Jean Jackson Hastings
NASHVILLE, TENNESSEE

Quick Tip
CAKE PLATE

A month before her daughter's fourth birthday, Lauri Campbell of Charlottesville, Virginia, took her to a ceramics shop, where she painted her very own Birthday Cake Plate, to be used each year at her party — a tradition she's since extended to include her son.

Neat Twist
BIRTHDAY PANCAKES

Stephanie Weight of Cedar Rapids, Iowa, carries on a tradition her own mother started. On birthday mornings, she makes pancakes for her kids (ages five, three, and eight months) and serves them with a lit birthday candle and a rousing rendition of "Happy Birthday."

King for the Day

Put the birthday child in charge with a one-day reign

"The birthday person in our family is king or queen for the day, complete with a crown if he or she is willing to wear it. **The royalty chooses all meals and decides what kind of cake we will have. He or she is released from all household chores for the day and even controls the television remote.** The King or Queen can also choose a family activity, such as going to the park or playing games."

—Dianne White

RICHMOND, VIRGINIA

A birthday crown lets everyone know who's boss.

Neat Twist

TOGETHER TIME

When their older daughter was turning three, the Jacques family of Yucca Valley, California, decided that their gift to her would be to go someplace special as a family for the day. They've continued the tradition throughout the years, and mom Tami says both her daughters love it. "They enjoy deciding where we should go, and we enjoy spending time with them," she says.

Sibling Gift

A present from the birthday child keeps jealousy at bay

"On my daughter's birthday, **she gives her brother a small but thoughtful gift with a loving note saying how glad she is to have him.** He does the same for her on his birthday. We did it for them when they were little, but now that they are in their teens, they are very excited to do it on their own."

— Mary Harris
SUMMERVILLE, SOUTH CAROLINA

Quick Tip

CREATE A SLEEP-OVER KIT

Jode Brexa of Boulder, Colorado, presented her niece, Madison, with a "welcome to Auntie's" sleepover kit on her fifth birthday: a floral-print shoe box stocked with pajamas and fancy toiletries. The kit stays at Jode's house so it's always ready and waiting.

Neat Twist

CLASS PRESENT

Instead of taking birthday cupcakes to school, the Adams children of San Jose, C a gift for their classroom. The wrapped present — usually a book or supplies birthday child in front of their classmates and presented to all of them.

Annual Letters

Dad's literary tradition records a year's worth of memories

"My husband writes a letter to our daughter every year for her birthday. He started this tradition while we were waiting for Abby's birth. He wrote to her about his dreams and fears, and his anticipation of the delivery. These days, **Dad's letters to Abby tell of her accomplishments over the year, his hopes for the coming year, and a little about us as a family.** We read the previous letters to her around her birthday."

—Katie Olson

DES MOINES, IOWA

alifornia, bring
— is opened by the

s' birthdays, the Sprecaceneres of Palm Bay, Florida,
nd cinnamon toast. As each family member tells the birth-
n or her, mom Pamela writes it down on paper in gold ink.
envelope, sealed by each of them with a lipstick kiss, then
e box with a vow not to open it until he or she turns eighteen.

Birthday Book

A special notebook tracks changes through the years

"Each of our children (ages eighteen, sixteen, and thirteen) has a birthday notebook. In it, **they list their current friends, favorite subjects at school, what they want to be when they grow up, and their height and weight.** We include birthday photos and a description of the day's festivities and invite party guests to autograph it. The children enjoy going back through their books to find happy memories."

—Lea Boyd

WALES, WISCONSIN

Annual entries keep this book fresh.

Birthday Tree

Chart your child's growth with a dedicated planting

"For our daughter's first birthday, we planted a tree and we took a picture of her standing next to it. **Every year since, we have taken a picture of her next to her tree.** We have since planted a tree for our son, too."

—Jennifer Tucker

MEDINA, OHIO

Quick Tip

HANG A HEIGHT CHART

When a birthday rolls around in the Ryan household of Ontario, Canada, it's time to visit the family's height chart, where the birthday child's new stature is marked in a preassigned color, and a year's worth of growth celebrated.

Neat Twist

WATCHING TIME FLY

Every year around their daughter's birthday, the Kuglers of Orlando, Florida, videotape her sitting in the same chair for several seconds. They plan to show the video on fast-forward when she's an adult and watch her grow up before their eyes.

"I'm Five" Cookie

Take a birthday photo with an edible prop

"In our family, we have a special birthday tradition. **My mom bakes number-shaped cookies for her grandchildren on their birthdays.** I always take a picture of my kids holding up one of their cookies. This is a fun way to mark the passing of time, and the kids can't wait to get their cookies from 'Yiayia.'"

—Stacey Duggar

TALLAHASSEE, FLORIDA

Stacey's daughter Rachel poses for her fifth-year photo.

Neat Twist

FINGER PHOTO

On each child's birthday, the Mulvilles of Cape May, New Jersey, take a photo of the celebrant holding up as many fingers as they are years old. That way, says mom Maria, "When we look back, we will always know what age they are in the 'finger photo.'"

Countdown Paper Chain

Simple links mark the days until a new sibling arrives

"When I was pregnant with my daughter, Savannah, my two sons, Sam, age six, and Noah, four, would incessantly ask me, 'When is our sister coming?' To help them understand that she couldn't be rushed, **I had them make a pink-and-white paper chain with 100 links, one for each day until the baby was due.** Every night, they would take turns cutting a link off the chain. It showed them just how much time it takes for a baby to be born."

Noah, left, and Sam kept count of when their baby sister was due.

—**Lauren Stadtlander**

PEMBROKE PINES, FLORIDA

Handprint Blanket

Help siblings create a warm welcome for a new arrival

"After a new baby was born in our neighborhood, I wanted to do something special. So I enlisted his two sisters in making a gift for him. **First, I sewed a baby blanket out of solid-color flannel. Then, using fabric paint, I had Eleah, age four, and Paige, three, personalize it with hand- and footprints.** I topped it off by spelling out 'My Big Sisters Love Me' with stick-on letters that we used as stencils, sponging fabric paint around them. Baby Brother and Mom loved it!"

—**Kelly Clark**
BOTHELL, WASHINGTON

Kelly's daughter Rowenna, left, helped pals Eleah and Paige make a blanket for their new brother.

Neat Twist

HOMEMADE STORY TAPE

As a special welcome for her first niece, Amy Bartlett of Hallsville, Missouri, recorded her seven-year-old daughter, Hadley, reading a book they'd bought for the baby. Hadley and her brother, Parker, four, then made a label for the cassette case by decorating a piece of card stock with the book title and some drawings. It was such a hit, it's now a family new-baby tradition.

Back-to-School Book

A homemade journal gets kids geared up for class

"During the final week of our summer break last year, I realized that my four- and six-year-olds needed a project to help get them in a back-to-school mind-set. **I bought two three-ring binders with clear plastic sheaths on the front and suggested they each make a book about starting class.** For the covers, they decorated title pages to slip under the plastic. For the inside pages, I printed simple work sheets from the computer with headings such as 'What I'll wear on the first day' and 'My new backpack.' The kids filled in the pages with drawings and notes. We made other pages for them to complete after school started, such as 'Something funny that happened today was . . .' and 'I was so happy when I found out that . . . .' They both ended up looking forward to the start of school so they could finish their books."

—Debbie Swanson
WESTFORD, MASSACHUSETTS

Capture the Day on Video

An annual walking, talking record lets kids reflect on changes

Each year, Susanne Boss of Massillon, Ohio, videotapes her kids as they get ready on the first day of school. While Taylor, age nine, and Corey, six, brush their teeth and eat breakfast, **Susanne asks them about their hopes and worries. A year later, a night or two before school begins again, they all watch the previous year's video.** "They get a kick out of looking at how much they've grown," says Susanne. "And they know the answers to some of the things they might have feared or wondered about." Most of all, she says, "It reminds them of the fun they had last year and how there really wasn't anything to be worried about."

Neat Twist
PHOTO SIGN

On the first day of school every year, the Gordon kids — and Sarah — of Allison Park, Pennsylvania, each pose with a sign proclaimi Grade," along with the date. The tradition is so strong that for Randy party, mom Mary was able to make a collage of all his annual

Kindergarten Party

An early celebration gets kids ready for the start of school

"A group of us whose daughters were all starting kindergarten decided to throw a Welcome to Kindergarten party. Each mom was responsible for bringing a craft project and something for the group's lunch. **At the party, the girls made photo albums, decorated first-day-of-school picture frames, painted their nails, and made bracelets.** For lunch, we put small cups of fruit and vegetables, sandwiches, salads, and cookies out on the table, and the girls took cafeteria trays and made their selections. After lunch, we had a backpack relay race during which the girls loaded backpacks with school supplies they then got to keep. The party gave our daughters a chance to meet new friends and learn new things."

—Joanne Mamenta Bjordahl
NASHVILLE, TENNESSEE

Randy, Jr., Brian,
"First Day of ___
's high-school graduation
photos, right through 12th grade.

Going-to-School Party before each child's first day of
t includes close friends and family members, cake, decora-
ngs like a backpack, a lunch box, school supplies,
tive atmosphere helps her kids look forward to school.

Throw a Bus-stop Bash

A first-morning party brings the neighborhood together

Every year on the first day of school, the **Suits of Zeeland, Michigan,** throw a breakfast bash at the bus stop by their driveway. The four kids in the family send invitations ahead of time to all the other riders in their neighborhood. **The night before school begins, mom Diane uses sidewalk chalk to draw pictures and messages on the pavement and hauls their picnic table to the end of the driveway.** The next morning, she adds balloons and sets the table with juice, muffins, and doughnuts. When the children arrive, they snack, visit, and add their own chalk decorations as they wait for the bus. When it arrives, there's one more surprise in store. Says Diane, "We always make up a little plate for the bus driver, too."

For a moveable feast, try using a child's wagon as a serving cart.

Chalkboard Cake

Welcome kids home from their first day with a neat treat

"When I was a child, **the best part of the first day of school was my mom's Blackboard Cake, a sheet cake with smooth chocolate frosting.** She'd use white icing to write ABCs and draw on it. I remember running to tell Mom all about my day while enjoying cake and milk. I've continued this tradition with my daughters and love experiencing with them the same excitement I shared with my mom."

The Stark's back-to-school snack takes the cake.

—Jane Stark

PLYMOUTH, MINNESOTA

Get-to-Know-You Tea

Invite your child's teacher to your home for a visit

"We have a wonderful back-to-school tradition of inviting our children's teachers to tea. It all started when my daughter, Kate, then a new preschool student, asked if we could invite her teacher to play at our house! While my first impulse was to tell her no, after thinking about it for a moment, I said why not? It's a great way for Kate, now age eight, and David, seven, to really connect with their teachers. **The hour or so that we spend having tea together allows me to get to know the people with whom my children spend such a large**

part of their day. It also helps them to see my kids as individuals, and to see me as something other than a voice on the phone or a name on the notes I send to school."

Talk with your child's teacher over a cup of tea.

—Tammy Zurawski
STRONGSVILLE, OHIO

Quick Tip

WRITE A LETTER OF INTRODUCTION Shannon Riggs of Victoria, British Columbia, sends her kids off to school on the first day with letters of introduction. The notes tell teachers when and how Shannon would like to volunteer and share a little about Sabrina, age ten, and Jake, eight.

Videotape Everyday Life

Simple activities make for a priceless record

When **Carla Poulin's** brother-in-law asked for a tape of her sons, Ryan and Tyler, ages four and six, the **Randolph, New Jersey,** mom decided to skip the usual Christmas or birthday videos and make one that captured their everyday life. The result was such a hit that **Carla now plays filmmaker twice a year, trailing her kids as they eat breakfast, ride bikes, take gymnastics class, show off new toys, and generally go about the business of growing up.** Not only do these 30-minute videos keep doting relatives up-to-date on Poulin family life, they also have claimed top billing at home. "We watch them all the time," says Carla, laughing. "My husband and I get all nostalgic about how much our children have grown, while the boys just sit there cracking up at each other. It's way better than television."

Capture a typical day in your home with a video diary.

Memory Boxes

Collect each child's mementos in a special container

"I've made a special keepsake box for each of my kids, Austin, age six, Breanna, four, and Cassandra, two. **In each one, I've included their baby book, my pregnancy journal, and another journal in which I've written cute things each child has said and done over the years.** I've also asked relatives to write letters to put into the boxes; family members too young to write have drawn a picture or made a craft to contribute instead. We plan on adding to these treasure chests for years to come and presenting them to our kids on their sixteenth birthdays."

—Vikki Wischhoefer

POULSBO, WASHINGTON

Make a Family Cookbook

Blend recipes and recollections for a keepsake you can really use

Tastes and smells — whether of Dad's famous pancakes or a savory Thanksgiving turkey — are powerful reminders of people, places, and good times. To create a culinary history of her family, **Terrie Shortsleeve** of **Shaw Air Force Base, South Carolina,** collected her handwritten recipe cards, photos, and recipe memories in a 6- by 6-inch scrapbook. "My seven-year-old daughter loves looking at the Family Cookbook," notes Terrie. **"It helps her help me pick out what to make for dinner, and at the same time reinforces her ties to friends and family."**

Mini Photo Albums

Small, themed books make organizing pictures a snap

"I was fed up with my big, disorganized family photo albums. It was a chore to arrange all the pictures on a page, and after all that work, the books still didn't always make sense. **So I bought a bunch of 4- by 6-inch mini albums that hold just a few dozen photos each and assigned them themes, such as 'Summer in Maine' or 'Danyelle's Graduation.'** Now I can arrange my favorite photos quickly, and I always know where to find them. Some albums, like 'Christmas Morning,' are ongoing, and I add a few pictures every year. When you flip through that one, the kids seem to grow up right before your eyes."

—Ginger Barr Heafey

NORTHAMPTON, MASSACHUSETTS

Keep it together with pint-sized albums.

Shadow-box Mementos

A photo with souvenirs makes an eye-catching display

"During our visit to Maine, my children, Michaela, age two, and Robert, five, were thrilled when they found little treasures that had washed ashore, such as shells, sand dollars, crab claws, and sea glass. When we returned home, Robert wanted to do something to display his collection and preserve the memories of this special vacation. **We decided to mount an 8- by 10-inch picture of him on a piece of foam board, then glue the ocean mementos right onto the photo.** Finally, we taped the whole thing into a clear plastic shadow-box frame."

—Judy Butzberger-Traitz

DAVIE, FLORIDA

Robert with his
3-D keepsake.

Time in a Bottle

Vacation memories are just a stone's throw away with these jarred treasures

"Our kids (Kiersten, age twelve, Nicolai, ten, Jarin, four, and Micah, one) love to collect rocks, so whenever we go someplace special, we choose one to mark the trip. **We write on them — where we went, the date, the initials of those who were there, and other notes, if there is room — and save them in glass jars.** We love looking at the rocks and remembering the places we've been and the people who were with us. Memories of Sunday drives, camping trips, fairs, birthday parties, and family vacations are all recorded and bottled."

The Clawson family's rock collection.

—Ron and Marci Clawson

SANDY, UTAH

Create Photo Place Mats

Laminate a photo collage and enjoy your memories every day

A homemade photo place mat crowded with good friends and summer memories can keep your family company all year round. "We made ours with photos from our annual summer vacation with close friends to the beach," says **Jemma Craig** of **Jamestown, Rhode Island.** "The kids have so much fun looking at the pictures — and it's a great way to remember our incredible vacation."

Have your memories and eat from them, too, with a keepsake place mat.

Crafting these couldn't be easier: first, arrange photos on an 11- by 17-inch sheet of paper. Then color-copy as many as you need (about $2 each) **and laminate them** (about another $3 each). [Tip: Be sure to use color copies; the heat from laminating can distort real photos. To fit in more photos, arrange them on a 16- by 20-inch sheet, then have it reduced to 11 by 17 inches.]

Ring of Postcards

Notes to yourself make a simple travel gallery

"My family loves to travel, and I have found a wonderful way to preserve our vacation memories. First, we buy postcards at all the different locations we visit. On the backs, I jot down the highlights of the trip or funny things that happened while we were there. After we have returned home, **I laminate all the postcards, punch holes in the top left corners, and put them all on a ring clip.** It's exciting to see all of the places we have been, and the cards are inexpensive souvenirs of our travels."

—**Stefanie Wirths**
CAMDENTON, MISSOURI

Quick Tip

GIVE CAMERAS TO THE KIDS

Instead of buying souvenirs on a trip to San Francisco, Darleen Stowell of Reno, Nevada, gave each of her kids (ages fourteen, nine, and four) a disposable camera so they could record their own vacation memories. They were excited to see the results, and the youngest collected hers in a notated photo album.

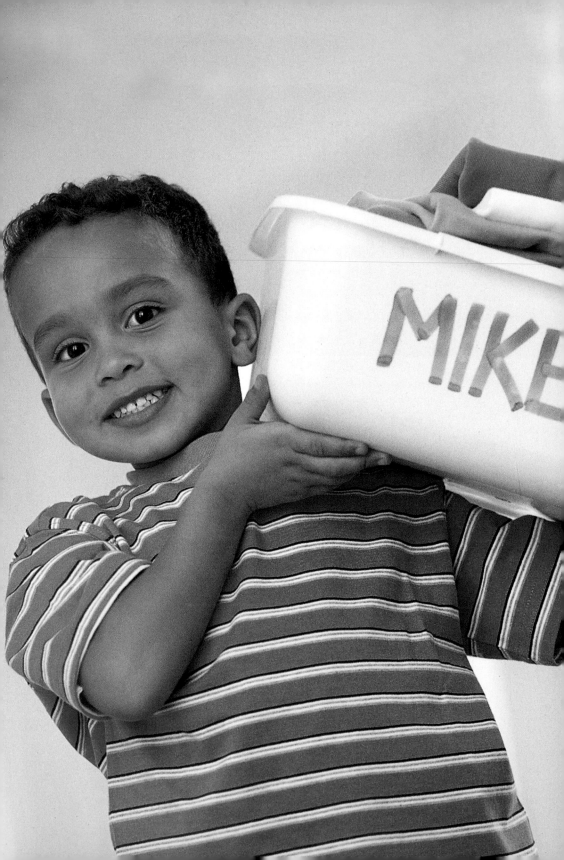

Chapter 6

Family Home

Clever ideas for organizing clutter and creating kid-friendly spaces that work for the whole family

If you need a reminder that family is a powerful thing, consider how quickly even a modest-sized one can reduce an orderly house to a witch's brew of toys, laundry, and misplaced school papers. We know that a home should be a place of peace where family members can express their personality, interests, and creativity. We also know it's hard to make that happen unless you have a handle on the chaos. In this chapter, *FamilyFun* readers share their best do-it-yourself ideas for bringing order to your household and customizing your space to fit your family's style. Best of all, every one of these projects is affordable. Now that's the kind of home improvement we think everyone can appreciate.

Contents

224 **Controlling Clutter**

236 **Kids' Bedrooms**

240 **Decorating**

242 **Displaying Kids' Artwork**

246 **Laundry & Clothing**

248 **Bathrooms**

Set up a Mini Mudroom

Ready-to-use shelving creates an easy organizer

It took less than two hours for the **Willemses** of **Brookline, Massachusetts,** to create a compact mudroom in a laundry area just beyond their front door.

A prefinished solid-wood shelving unit is anchored to a stud in the wall, with shelves placed strategically to serve as storage and seating (the seats are braced with sturdy L brackets). Hooks are mounted along horizontal wood strips to catch coats and hats. See-through boxes, clearly labeled, keep sunglasses, library books, and spare change tidy; wicker baskets store foul-weather gear and out-of-season sports equipment; and shoes and boots slide under the bottom shelf.

Quick Tip

PUT IT OUT OF SIGHT

To get rid of clutter, Tish Keating Skaronea of Lake Bluff, Illinois, recommends boxing up all the junk you don't know what to do with and putting it somewhere out of the way for a month. "If you don't miss it, don't open the boxes again," she says. "Take them out and donate them."

Catchall Baskets

Give each child a place to toss his downstairs clutter

"I have baskets throughout the house, one for each child, to stash things 'in transit.' Sometimes you're just too rushed to get that sweater back upstairs before soccer practice. **But there's one rule: at the end of the day, your basket needs to be emptied.**"

—Tara Aronson

PACIFIC PALISADES, CALIFORNIA

Neat Twist
STAIR ASSIGNMENTS
At the Parks household in Austin, Texas, everyone in the family of six is assigned a step at the bottom of the stairs. As belongings accumulate downstairs, they are sorted and piled on each person's step, to be returned to his or her room on the next trip upstairs. Laminated name tags hanging on the wall just above each step facilitate sorting and mean there are never unclaimed piles.

Refrigerator Pockets

Fabric organizer displays school papers and artwork

"Since I was once a kindergarten teacher, I knew to expect a lot of artwork and school papers when I sent my first child to kindergarten. In anticipation, I came up with a creative organizational system for the side of the refrigerator. **I sewed rectangles of fabric to a large piece of contrasting material, creating pockets big enough to hold standard-size papers as well as construction paper.** I hung the organizer on the refrigerator with magnetic clips from a local hardware store. Ryan takes great pleasure in displaying his papers, and I am thrilled that we can do it in an organized fashion."

—Amy Davis
LEVEL GREEN, PENNSYLVANIA

This handy organizer lets Ryan (with little sister Courtney) show off his work.

Neat Twist

ACCORDION FILE

To organize her fourth-grader's exploding collection of school papers, Kim Donahue of Absecon, New Jersey, purchased a plastic accordion folder in a hip neon color and helped him carefully label each file. It's been so successful, Kim says, "half the class have them now."

Designate In and Out Boxes

Keep track of papers with personalized office trays

With five kids ages eighteen months to twenty years, the Finnegans of Richmond, Virginia, were drowning in paperwork. Their solution? A set of office-style in and out boxes, labeled for each family member. **Any papers the kids need their parents to check or sign — such as homework, report cards, permission slips, and the like — must be put in an in box.** Says mom Terri, "The children have really assumed responsibility. We no longer turn the house upside down looking for papers, and we've even stopped misplacing them ourselves."

Neat Twist
PERSONAL BINDERS

Tanya Beeler of Hillsboro, Oregon, keeps a binder for each of her three kids, its dividers labeled with headings like Activities, School, and Sports. "Any papers that I get for each child have their own place to go," says Tanya, "and if I need to find out what time the next game is, I know where to look."

Library-Book Bag

Keep your kids' library books in check with a custom tote

"My five-year-old son, Eric, would routinely put away his library books with his own books, and they were impossible to find when it came time to return them. To fix this problem, **we bought Eric a small tote bag and labeled it 'Eric's Library Books.' We punched a hole through the corner of his library card, looped a piece of string through it, and tied it to his bag to keep him from losing it.** When we visit the library, Eric can check out only as many books as he can fit in his bag, and when we get home, he makes sure the library books stay in the bag when they are not being read, to keep from misplacing them."

—Marquesa Fedastion
COLORADO SPRINGS, COLORADO

Eric with his personalized tote bag.

Rotate Books Monthly

Selections stay fresh with revolving boxes

When it comes to books, the Stovall family of Roswell, Georgia, finds that absence really does make the heart grow fonder. It also makes the house tidier. **The Stovalls store a portion of their book collection in Books of the Month Boxes — cardboard magazine holders filled with seasonal reads.** They simply labeled a box for each month, then loaded it with topical favorites. The September box, for example, holds books about school, apples, and autumn. The boxes are stored in a closet until each makes its annual month-long appearance. Five-year-old Ava, the eldest of the three Stovall girls, can't wait to flip the calendar page and announce, "Time to get out a new box of books!"

Use magazine holders to store off-season books out of sight.

Toy Checkout

An "on loan" system helps keep playthings in order

"The toy room in our house was constantly a disaster, so I came up with a way to help my daughters, Taylor, age nine, and Abbey, five, learn to keep it neat and organized. First, we installed shelves on the walls and in the closet, using masking tape to mark off a designated spot for each toy or game. Next, I painted three wooden sticks for each child, which we store in a juice can by the toy-room door. **The girls each have their own color sticks and use them to 'check out' the toys by setting one on the shelf in place of each toy they take out.** This system works great: we can tell right away who has taken out what, and the toy room is never a mess anymore."

—**Susy Curtis**
ORLANDO, FLORIDA

Quick Tip

TACKLE 10 ITEMS AT A TIME

Julie Semlak of Normal, Illinois, swears by the 10-Thing Rule. "If there's a massive pile of kids' toys, sort through ten," she says. "It's easy to deal with anything if it's broken into smaller bits and you've given yourself permission ahead of time not to do it all at once."

Use Picture Labels

Photos on storage boxes show nonreaders where toys should go

To help her preschool daughters keep their toys organized, Julie Filbeck of Auburn, Washington, created a set of simple storage boxes labeled with both pictures and words. To start, **Julie covered a set of cardboard boxes with decorative Con-Tact paper and grouped like toys inside each one.** Then she took a close-up photo of a few items from each box, glued the pictures onto white paper,

labeled them with bold markers, laminated them, and attached them to the boxes with clear packing tape. The picture-box system also helped when other kids came to play. Says Julie, "They'd look at the pictures, and then they'd get the necklaces back into the necklace box, the Barbies in the Barbie box, and the horses in the horse box."

Grouping like items together makes cleaning up a snap.

Mini Museums

Under-the-bed storage boxes display kids' collections

"My five children's collections of rocks, coins, shells, and other treasures were beginning to take over the house, so we came up with a new way to store and display them. **I purchased under-the-bed boxes — one each for my older kids and a shared one for my two youngest to start — and suggested they turn them into museums for their favorite things.** They all thought it was a wonderful idea and frequently pull them out to show to visitors."

Dana's daughter Sarah displays a few of her prized-possessions.

—Dana Lowry

HICKORY, NORTH CAROLINA

Trinket Box

Glue tiny treasures to a special container

"My two daughters, Kierston, age five, and Kelsey, six, enjoy collecting very small toys, but I am always stepping on them and then tossing them in the garbage, much to the girls' chagrin. **In an effort to save their toys and keep them from getting underfoot, I made the girls a trinket box.** I had them gather up all their little toys and used a glue gun to attach the toys to the outside of an empty box. The girls love this solution, and they can store their ongoing collections inside."

Kierston's tiny toys now have a home, thanks to this handsome holder.

—Connie Cannon
CARLSBAD, CALIFORNIA

Neat Twist
BIG-SISTER BOX

To keep unsuitable toys away from her one-year-old, MacGregor, without penalizing his big sister, Mallory, Rachel Roberts of Berea, Kentucky, filled a large plastic storage bin with the offending items and stashed it on the top shelf of the toy closet. The Big Sister Box only comes down when MacGregor is napping, and makes Mallory feel extra special.

Portable Dress-up Closet

Transform an oversize box into a play wardrobe

"My daughters, Chandler, six, and Kelsey, two, just love to play dress-up. **The sight of their clothes all wrinkled up in a box drove me crazy, so we made each of the girls a portable closet from cardboard boxes.** (One is a garment box we had left over from our last move.) We cut openings for the clothes and shoes, added bars for hanging, and covered them with Con-Tact paper. We also added stick-on hooks to the outsides for holding necklaces, scarves, and handbags. Our dress-up boxes are economical, practical, and fun!"

Kelsey and Chandler each have a wardrobe fit for a princess.

—Robin Giese

TRAPPE, PENNSYLVANIA

Neat Twist

THREE-SHELF DOLLHOUSE

Carol Forsyth of Eagan, Minnesota, created a dollhouse for her daughter, Sydney, out of stackable plastic shelves. For the facade, she decorated a piece of cardboard with windows, doors, and flowers. Then she wallpapered the other side with scrapbook and wrapping papers and glued the whole thing to the shelving.

Stuffed-Animal Hanger

A column of hooks keeps furry friends organized

"My husband and I found a fun and practical way to display our son's ever-growing collection of stuffed animals. **We mounted a seven-foot piece of furring strip to the wall in a corner of our playroom, then added mug hooks every six inches.** Nicholas, age three, then selected his favorite animals for display, which we hung up by their ribbons or arms, creating both a storage solution and an eye-catching decoration."

—Karen Langford

ERIE, PENNSYLVANIA

Nicholas Langford and his pals have a new hangout.

Neat Twist
PLUSH PALS SHOE BAG

To keep her daughter Madeline's flock of stuffed animals out from underfoot, Vicki Watson of Columbus, Ohio, herded them all into a shoe organizer. Now all of her daughter's favorite bears and bunnies have a room of their own while remaining visible to — and reachable by —Madeline.

Padded Ladder

Prevent stubbed toes with a pair of soft slippers

"My sons, Michael, age eleven, and Kevin, eight, love their bunk beds, but the ladder was a toe-stubbing hazard. **That problem was solved by having the ladder 'wear' a cushy pair of slippers!"**

—Jeannette Colgan

DREXEL HILL, PENNSYLVANIA

A bunk-bed ladder that won't bang your toes.

Neat Twist

BED-CURTAIN STREAMERS

When her daughter asked for a canopy bed, Helen Murdock-Prep of Huntington, New York, invited her to pick out six rolls of colorful paper streamers at a local party store instead. Mom and daughter then cut the streamers in strips and taped them to the ceiling around the side and foot of the bed. The result? A vibrant curtain that took 15 minutes to make and cost only $8.

Make a Chalkboard Dresser

Add fun to function by covering drawers with special paint

Mary Minter of Wauwatosa, Wisconsin, created a

prominent place for her son, Miles, to practice drawing and

writing by painting the drawers of an old bureau with

chalkboard paint. **"Now that he's older, dressing himself**

and learning to read, he can have his drawers labeled,"

says Mary, who likes the educational aspect of her design.

For extra zip, and to accent the drawers, she added

red stripes to the front. [Tip: Use a wet

washcloth, rather than an eraser, to wipe

scribblings clean.]

Miles knows where
everything goes.

Alligator Dimmer Switch

Liven up the light switch by gluing on a small toy

"For my son Henry's room, **I used epoxy to attach a plastic toy alligator to the dimmer switch.** Even when the lights are low, this swampy-green critter gets lots of attention, and I'm convinced it helps all of us remember to turn off the lights when we leave the room."

A snappy switch reminds everyone to turn off the light.

—Sharon Miller Cindrich

WAUWATOSA, WISCONSIN

Quick Tip

TURN RAIN GUTTERS INTO BOOKSHELVES

The Meliezers of Douglasville, Georgia, attached a 5-foot length of vinyl rain gutter to the wall in each of their kids' rooms to store and display their many books. The gutters can be installed easily using the hanging brackets sold with them.

Paint a Handprint Border

Let kids have a hand in personalizing their space

To liven up the decor in her sons' room, **Michelle Outland** of **Sun Valley, Nevada,** invited Quin, age six, and Andrew, five, to

Quin and Andrew demonstrate how they decorated their wall — and each other.

create a colorful border of handprints. First, she stuck masking tape on the wall to mark the top and bottom edges of the border. Then **she brushed their hands with primary colors of latex paint and guided them to the proper spot.** An added bonus? They gained an easy way to mark their growth. The boys still know which prints are theirs, and, Michelle says, "we occasionally measure to see how much bigger their hands are today."

Neat Twist
CREATE WALLPAPER CUTOUTS

To add a whimsical touch to their six-year-old daughter's room, Martin and Angie Fox of Hartsville, South Carolina, cut out fairy figures from a prepasted wallpaper border, dunked them in water, and stuck them all over the walls in expected, and unexpected, spots.

Paper a Wall with Postcards

Turn mementos into an inexpensive conversation piece

Susanne Barkan hated the big, white wall in her **Shelburne Falls, Massachusetts,** dining room, so while her husband, Craig Miller, was out of town, she and her five-year-old son, Ben, surprised him by **creating a wall "quilt" from their postcard collection.** "Ben took care of the bottom rows; I did the top ones," Susanne says. Not only does the display provide hours of conversation, it's also a great entertainment center. "We play games like I Spy and Spot the Categories," says Susanne.

Ben, top, in front of his family's "quilt" made from 350 postcards.

Quick Tip

DECORATE BLINDS WITH STICKERS

To liven up a set of plain white blinds in their Mansfield, Texas, home, Susan Hanson and her daughter, Haley, age eleven, covered them with large flower stickers. They attached the stickers with the blinds closed, then Susan used an X-Acto knife to cut each one between the slats.

Limited Editions

Welcome a new sibling with special paintings

"When I was expecting our third child, my husband and I wanted to involve our daughter, Jillian, age four, and son, Kevin, two, in the preparations. Since they both love to paint, **we set them loose at the easel with poster paints in the colors of the baby's room and hung their creations in the nursery.** Jillian and Kevin were able to help welcome their baby sister, and she got some special artwork for her room."

Jillian's and Kevin's designs adorn their new sister's room.

—**Susan Fields**
ST. CHARLES, MISSOURI

Neat Twist
COLOR-COORDINATED FAMILY ART

Using prestretched canvases, acrylic paints, and foam brushes, the McDearmonts of Highland Village, Texas, created a set of abstract paintings that complement the vibrantly colored furniture in their den. The works are unsigned. "Visitors have so much fun looking for images in the paintings and guessing who made each one," says mom DeAnna.

Paint Frames on the Wall

Create an eye-catching museum of ever-changing exhibits

To create a prominent gallery for her kids' achievements, Joceyln Robinson of Troy, Michigan, painted dozens of decorative faux frames right onto a stairwell wall. She hangs up whatever current awards or artwork her kids are most proud of, regularly rotating new papers onto this colorful wall of honor. **To make the frames, Jocelyn marked off masking-tape rectangles along the painted wall, using variously sized school art papers as a guide.** She painted the inside of each white, removed the masking tape, and then painted showy frames around them, employing every creative technique she could think of, including sponge printing, geometric prints, and thumbprint hearts and flowers. She uses double-sided tape to hang up the kids' work.

Permanent frames make it easy to display new masterpieces.

Bulletin-Board Frames

Wooden frames backed with foam core provide an easy
way to rotate artwork

"My daughters, Hilary, age fourteen, Gretchen,
twelve, and Brenda, nine, bring home so much art that
I thought it would be nice to set up a rotating gallery
that I could update with the latest pieces. However,
the varying sizes and shapes of their work made it
difficult to find frames that could accommodate this
idea. **I solved the problem by hot-gluing pieces of foam
core to the backs of various large, open wooden frames,
available at department stores or even at flea markets and
tag sales.** Now I use pushpins to mount the art on
the foam core and can change it anytime I feel like it,
putting in almost any piece of art they make —
even the three-dimensional stuff that wouldn't fit
under glass."

—Pamela Waterman

MESA, ARIZONA

Tabletop Gallery

Show off your child's creations on the kitchen table

"Not long after my daughter, Mikayla, started kindergarten, we realized we didn't have enough room on our refrigerator for all of her artwork. So instead of cluttering the fridge, **we lay them on top of our kitchen table, then cover them with a clear plastic tablecloth held tight with picnic-table clips.** This way, we can enjoy viewing her special works without any hassle."

—Rebeccah Doggett
ELLINGTON, CONNECTICUT

Mikayla with her tabletop display.

Neat Twist
UNDER GLASS
Suzanne Grocki of South Burlington, Vermont, had a piece of glass cut to fit the top of the family's kitchen table. Photographs, drawings, and sketches are slipped underneath for easy viewing.

My Art Book

One photo preserves weeks of work

"My eight-year-old son, Braden, brings home a ton of art projects from school every week. We love them all, but keeping every one would create quite a storage issue. To cut down on the stacks of artwork but still preserve the memories, we created a special album. **At the end of each month, Braden poses for a picture surrounded by that month's worth of his work.** Then we save a few of his favorite pieces and toss the rest. We add the pictures to his book to document his projects over the year."

Braden poses with his creations for his monthly picture.

—**Vicki Banfield**
MARSHALL, MICHIGAN

Neat Twist
PERSONALIZED PORTFOLIOS
To help keep track of her kids' artwork, Marleen Montgomery of Gaithersburg, Maryland, made portfolios out of large pieces of cardboard bound together with fabric and tape. Each child decorated hers with photos and magazine pictures.

Sort into Stackable Drawers

Let each family member carry their own laundry upstairs

Tired of the piles of laundry that always seemed to stretch across her bed, Jackie Lawrence of Omaha, Nebraska, came clean with the help of four stackable plastic drawers — one for each member of the family, labeled accordingly. **Folded laundry goes into the drawers, then it's up to the drawer's owner to fetch it and put it away.** The system's unexpected bonus: eight-year-old Reigan actually looks forward to checking her drawer for freshly washed clothes.

Removable drawers are easy to fill and transport.

Neat Twist
DESIGNATED DISHPANS

Borrowing an idea from her own mom, Krista Gafkjen of Panora, Iowa, folds the laundry into labeled plastic dishpans, one for each family member. Even two-year-old KC can take her bin up to her room and put away her own socks, notes Krista.

Under-the-Bed Bins

Easily accessible boxes keep hand-me-downs organized

"Because my boys are only a year apart, we need a hand-me-down-clothes system that is right at our disposal. I bought a plastic under-the-bed bin — we like the ones with wheels — and labeled it the size my younger son, Nick, is quickly outgrowing. **When I see an article of clothing is too small, I add it to the bin under his bed; when the bin gets full, I give away the contents to a friend with a younger child.** Meantime, I put all the clothes his older brother, Jack, outgrows right into Nick's dresser. For those sentimental items I can never part with, I have a special bin under my own bed that says, 'Kid Clothes Never to Give Away.'"

Label boxes by size for simple sorting.

—**Alexandra Kennedy**

NORTHAMPTON, MASSACHUSETTS

Tote Your Toiletries

Individual carryalls help ease bathroom gridlock

Sue Davis of **Sycamore, Illinois,** keeps each family member's toiletries in a separate basket (she favors plastic-coated metal). That way, **when one bathroom is occupied, it's easy to carry what you need to the other.**

Plus, cleaning is much simpler: you just lift up a few baskets, instead of maneuvering dozens of oozy bottles and tubes to scrub under them. Sue credits her mother with the idea. "I grew up with three sisters — four girls, four girl teenagers, all of us in the bathroom at the same time. My mom had to think of something!"

Quick Tip

POCKET YOUR HAIR ACCESSORIES

Tammy Lindsay of Carrollton, Virginia, uses a clear, pocketed hanging organizer to keep daughter Chelsea's hair barrettes, ribbons, scrunchies, and bows sorted and within easy reach. Items are grouped by style and color.

Neat Twist

TACKLE BOX FOR HAIR TIES

Lisa Stovall of Roswell, Georgia, keeps her three daughters' hair accessories in a plastic tackle box. Barrettes, hair marbles, and bows all have their special place. "And when somebody wants pigtails," says Lisa, "we can actually find two hair ties that match."

Hand-Washing Play Station

Underwater treasure hunt makes a game of getting clean

"Getting our two-year-old son, Eli, to wash his hands before every meal was becoming a huge challenge, but I recently found a way to make it fun. **Before meals, I fill the sink with soapy water and drop in a few of his small toys.** Then I tell Eli there are treasures in the bottom of the sink for him to find. He's always excited to figure out what's hidden and ends up playing in the water for a few minutes."

—**Darcee Pantaz**

PORTLAND, MAINE

Quick Tip

COLOR-CODE YOUR TOWELS

With five children ranging in age from eight to nineteen, Carolyn McLaughlin of Sunnyvale, Texas, was tired of hearing "It's not mine" every time she found a towel on the floor or a dirty cup on the counter. So she assigned each child a color for frequently used objects, including towels, washcloths, cups, house keys, and school folders.

Index

A

Abstract Family Art, 241
Accordion File for papers, 226
Activities, see also *Backyard, Games, Fall, Spring, and Summer*
  Activity-a-Day Calendar, 120
  Activity Bingo, 134
  Bored Book, 84
  craft club, 85
  Idea Box, 84
  Indoor Safari, 87
  Project Bags, 85
  Toy Animal Zoo, 86
Adding Game, 151
Adventurous Eater, 45
After-School Icons, 20
Alligator Dimmer Switch, 238
allowance, Check Register, 153
Alphabet Anglers, 136
Angel Trails, 49
Annotated Map, 107
Annual getting ready for school video, 209
Annual (birthday) Letters, 202
Apple Print Shirts, 128
Apron, craft, 90
Artwork, kids
  Bulletin-Board Frames, 243
  My Art Book, 245
  painted frames on wall, 242
  Personalized Portfolios, 245
  Tabletop Gallery, 244
  Under Glass, 244
Autumn Maze, 127

B

Babies
  Baby Faces (family tree), 185
  Countdown Paper Chain, 206
  Handprint Blanket, 207
  Homemade Story Tape, 207
  Limited Editions (paintings), 241
Backpack Notes, 20
Backseat Organizer, 108
Back-to-School Book, 208

Backyard activities
  Bike Wash, 112
  Hopscotch Tiles, 113
  Lawn-mower Patterns, 122
  Name Game, 111
  Portable Rice Table, 114
  Rock Box, 114
  Sticker Tag, 110
  Wading Pool Garden, 117
  Wheelbarrow Sandbox, 115
Bag Lunch with a Prize, 26
Bathrooms
  Color-coded towels, 249
  Hair Accessories, 248
  Hand-Washing station, 249
  Tackle Box for Hair ties, 248
  Toiletries Tote, 248
Beach Golf, 124
Bedrooms
  Alligator Dimmer Switch, 238
  Bed-Curtain Streamers, 236
  Chalkboard Dresser, 237
  Handprint Border, 239
  Padded (bunk bed) Ladder, 236
  Wallpaper Cutouts, 239
Bedtime
  Angel Trails, 49
  Bedtime Paper Chain, 48
  Big Bed Night, 79
  Hug and Kiss Jar, 51
  Magic Mommy Dust, 49
  Mission: Lights Out, 47
  Monstrous Sounds, 50
  Nightly Check-off, 46
  Sounder Snoozing, 50
Big Sister Box, 233
Bike Wash, 112
Bingo (chore) board, 34
Birthdays
  Annual Letters, 202
  Birthday Book, 203
  Birthday Fairy, 198
  Birthday of the Month, 181
  Birthday Pancakes, 199
  Birthday Tree, 204
  Breakfast Treat, 199
  Cake Plate, 199
  Class Present, 201
  Festive Wake Up, 198

  Finger Photo, 205
  Growing Up Video, 204
  Height Chart, 204
  "I'm Five" Cookie, 205
  King for the Day, 200
  Love Note, 202
  Sibling Gift, 201
  Sleepover Kit, 201
  Together Time, 200
Blackout Nights, 79
Block Heads (with photos), 184
Books
  Book Budget, 153
  Books of the Month Boxes, 229
  Library-Book Bag, 228
  Rain Gutter Bookshelves, 238
Bored Book, 84
Boss for the Day, 55
Breakfast
  Birthday Pancakes, 199
  Breakfast (Birthday) treat, 199
  Breakfast (menu) Box, 19
  Breakfast for Dinner, 70
  Breakfast in Bed, 18
  Buffet (for breakfast), 18
  Morning Menus, 19
Brother Bank, 159
Brotherly Love, 56
Bulletin-board Frames, 243
Bus-stop Bash, 211

C

Cake Plate (for birthday), 199
Calendar, Color-Coded, 28
Calling (change-of-address) Cards, 176
Cameras for the kids, 221
Candlelight Dinners, 69
Can-Do Can, 96
Car Bingo, Customized, 106
Cardboard Clone, 97
Cardboard Guitars, 94
Caring Can (for charity), 195
Car-less errands, 67
Castles, Colorful, 98
Catchall Baskets, 225
Chain Mail, 182

Chalkboard Cake, 212
Chalkboard Dresser, 237
Check Register (allowance), 153
Chess Set, 104
Chores
    Bingo (chore) Board, 34
    Clean Clothes Relay, 39
    Laundry Lesson, 39
    List of Jobs for Hire, 36
    Perfect Place Mats, 40
    Place Cards with a Twist, 41
    Prize (task) Jar, 38
    Punch Card for Chores, 35
    Sweet Rewards, 36
    Table-Setting Tasks, 40
    Task Train, 35
    "Whoops" Board, 37
Class (birthday) Present, 201
Classmate Cards, 105
Clippings, Customized, 182
Clock, Customized, 15
Clock, Mock, 15
Clothing
    Clean Clothes Relay, 39
    Clothes Clone, 16
    Firefighter's Muster, 17
    Heat it Up, 12
    Week's Worth of Outfits, 16
Clutter
    Accordion File, 226
    Big Sister Box, 233
    Catchall Baskets, 225
    In and Out Boxes, 227
    Mini Mudroom, 224
    Personal Binders, 227
    Refrigerator Pockets, 226
    Stair Assignments, 225
Coach's thank you gift, 169
Collection of Compliments
    (T-shirt), 171
Communication, family
    E-mail Exchange, 62
    Letters from Afar, 63
    Rotating Diary, 62
    Talking Chair, 64
    Thankful Caterpillar, 65
    Three Good Things, 65
Community service
    Caring Can, 195
    Craft Bags (for hospital), 189
    Crafts with the Elderly, 189

Handprint Tiles (school
    fund-raiser), 194
Ice-cream Drive, 193
Little Brother for the Day,
    191
Meals on Wheels, 190
Nursing-home Angel, 188
Parties for Charity, 195
Sewing Party for shelter, 193
Sneakers for Kids, 192
Conversation Starter, 68
Cool It (with frozen fruit), 44
Countdown (for baby) Paper
    Chain, 206
Coupon Game, 33
Cousin Collage, 185
Crack-the-Code Game, 141
Crafts
    Can-do Can, 96
    Cardboard Clone, 97
    Cardboard Guitars, 94
    Colorful Castles, 98
    Craft Bags (for hospital), 189
    Craft club, 85
    Craft Kits, Homemade, 88
    Craft Supply Station, 89
    Crafts with the Elderly, 189
    Fabric-Painted Gloves, 101
    Fun House, 95
    Glitter Shakers, 91
    Homemade Paper Dolls, 99
    Life-size Portrait, 96
    Marker Cap Keeper, 91
    Mixed-up Animals, 99
    Project Boxes, 88
    Stamped Stains t-shirts, 101
    T-shirt Quilt, 100
    Tube Puppets, 98
    Very Crafty Apron, 90

D

Daily Routines
    Daily Flip Cards, 28
    Daily (paper) Triage, 29
    Day in the Life of Me, 10
    Illustrated morning check-
        list, 10
    Pocket Planner, 11
Day of Thanks, 167
Daylight Savings Party, 81

Decision (for dinner) Day, 43
Decorating
    Abstract Family Art, 241
    Limited Editions
        (paintings), 241
    Postcard Wall, 240
    Stickers for Blinds, 240
Dinner menu planning
    Decision Day, 43
    Recipe File of Favorites, 43
    Rotating Menu, 42
Dinner traditions
    Breakfast for Dinner, 70
    Candlelight Dinners, 69
    Conversation Starter, 68
    Finger-Food Buffet, 70
    History Dinner, 72
    Kids Cook Night, 71
    Leftover Café, 71
    Neighborhood Dinner, 73
    Talking Stick, 68
Doggy Wake-Up Call, 12
Dollhouse, Three-Shelf, 234
Do Nothing Day, 59
Door Decor (for grandparent),
    187
Door (busy) Sign, 37
Dressing
    Clothes Clone, 16
    Firefighters' Muster, 17
    Week's Worth of Outfits, 16
Dress-up Closet, Portable, 234
Drive-in Movie Cars, 77

E

Ekyndorn Day, 58
E-mail Exchange, 62
Errands
    Car-less Errands, 67
    Coupon Game, 33
    Perpetual (grocery) List, 32
    Where-We're-Going
        (errand) Map, 32
Everyday Life (video), 214

F

Fabric-Painted Gloves, 101
Fall activities
    Apple Print Shirts, 128

Autumn Maze, 127
Fall Fantasy Homes, 127
Leaf People, 126
Pumpkin Snowman, 129
Scarecrow-Making Party, 126
Trash-bag Snowman, 129
Family Adventure Day, 61
Family Awards Night, 162
Family Cookbook, 216
Family, extended
Baby Faces (family tree), 185
Birthday of the Month, 181
Block Heads (with photos), 184
Chain Mail, 182
Cousin Collage, 185
Customized Clippings, 182
Door Decor (for grandparent), 187
Familiar Faces (matching game), 184
Honor a Family Member Night, 181
Kids' Artwork (care package), 180
Monthly Mailings, 183
Papa's life board game, 186
Photo (postcard) Mailers, 180
Photo Stories, 186
Wall-to-wall (hospital) Visitors, 187
Family Days, special
Boss for the Day, 55
Brotherly Love, 56
Do Nothing Day, 59
Ekyndorn Day, 58
Family Adventure Day, 61
Happy Relationship Day, 54
Hometown Tourists, 60
Kid of the Day, 55
Sister Book, 56
Yes Day, 57
Family Dice, 105
Family Felt Board, 102
Family nights
Big Bed Night, 79
Blackout Nights, 79
Daylight Savings Party, 81
Drive-in Movie Cars, 77

Indoor camping, 80
Movie Masquerade, 76
Movie Night, Family, 76
Nighttime Treasure Walk, 78
Park-in (garage) Movie, 77
Radio Hour, Family, 75
Show and Share, 75
Slumber Party, Family, 80
Starry Campout, 81
Themed Evenings, 74
Weekend Plan, 74
Finger-Food Buffet, 70
Finger-Painting Fun, 93
Finger Photo, 205
Firefighters' Muster, 17
Fitness
Car-less errands, 67
Race Training, 66
Walking Circle, 67
Workout Routines, 66
Flower Hunt, 118
Foreign-Language Twister, 146
Form Letter (for teachers), 22
Framed Farewell, 179
Friday Flowers, 163
Friendship
Calling Cards, 176
Framed Farewell, 179
Friendly Gift Wrap, 178
Get-to-Know-You Guest Book, 177
Kids' Phone Book, 177
Pen-pals Kit, 176
Shared Scrapbook, 178
Fruit and Veggie Bingo, 44
Fun House, 95
Fun (no-TV) Zone, 31
Funny Pictures, 102
Furry Friends Shoe Bag, 235

G

Games
Car Bingo, Customized, 106
Chess Set, 104
Classmate Cards, 105
Family Dice, 105
Hopscotch Tiles, 113
Mileage Markers, 107
Name (ball) Game, 111
Sticker Tag, 110

Treasure Jar, 109
Get-to-Know-You Tea, 213
Gift Certificate (for teacher), 173
Glass-covered table gallery, 244
Glitter shakers, 91
Gloves, Fabric-Painted, 101
Gold Medal Books, 142
Good Fairy (for niceness), 160
Grassroots Stylist, 116
Growing up birthday video, 204
Guest Book, 177

H

Hair Accessories, 248
Handprint (baby) Blanket, 207
Handprint Border, 239
Handprint Tiles (school fundraiser), 194
Handprint (class) T-shirt, 170
Hand-washing Play Station, 249
Happy Relationship Day, 54
Healthy Eating (Rainbow Lunch), 24
Heartfelt Bag, 172
Hidden letters, 137
History Dinner, 72
Hogwarts Summer Academy, 121
Hometown Tourists, 60
Honor a Family Member Night, 181
Hopscotch Tiles, 113
Hug and Kiss Jar, 51

I

Ice-cream Drive, 193
Ice-cream Tasting Party, 123
Ice-globe Lanterns, 131
Idea Box, 84
"I'm Five" Cookie, 205
Imaginary Trip, 146
In and Out Boxes, 227
Indoor camping, 80
Indoor Safari, 87

K

Keepsakes
Everyday Life (video), 214
Family Cookbook, 216

Memory Boxes, 215
Mini Photo Albums, 217
Video Scrapbook, 214
Kid of the Day, 55
Kids' Artwork (care package), 180
Kids Cook Night, 71
Kids' Phone Book, 177
Kind Comments, 161
Kindergarten Party, 210
Kindness sharing, 163
King for the Day, 200
Knapsack Neatener, 23

L
Late-night Reading, 144
Laundry
Clean Clothes Relay, 39
Designated Dishpans, 246
Laundry Lesson, 39
Stackable (laundry) Drawers, 246
Lawn-mower Patterns, 122
Leaf People, 126
Learning activities
Activity Bingo, 134
Adding Game, 151
Alphabet Anglers, 136
Book Budget, 153
Check Register, 153
Crack-the-Code Game, 141
Foreign-Language Twister, 146
Gold Medal Books, 142
Hidden Letters, 137
Imaginary Trip, 146
Late-Night Reading, 144
math problems, 151
Measuring Wall, 150
Mom-Mart, 152
Money Tree, 135
Mother-Daughter Book Club, 143
Musical-note Bingo, 134
Reading aloud, 142
Reading Tent, 144
Science Lab, 149
Sidewalk Chalk Spelling, 138
Tabletop Map, 147

Trips as (reading) Treats, 145
Wall (alphabet) Stickers, 137
Weather Center, 148
Word Challenge, 140
Word Pitch Game, 139
Leftover Café, 71
Letter of Introduction, 213
Letters from Afar, 63
Library-Book Bag, 228
Life-size Portrait, 96
List of Jobs for Hire, 36
Little Brother for the Day, 191
Limited Editions paintings, 241
Love Note (birthday), 202
Lunches
Bag Lunch with a Prize, 26
Healthy Eating, 24
Lunch Money Budget, 25
Lunchtime Laughs, 27
Mystery (lunch) Treat, 26
Napkin of the Day, 27
Written Record, 24

M
Magic Mommy Dust, 49
Manners
Brother Bank, 159
Family Awards Night, 162
Friday Flowers, 163
Good Fairy (for niceness), 160
Kind Comments, 161
Kindness sharing, 163
manners catchphrases, 157
Manners Game, 157
Manners Quiz, 158
No-Fear Dinners, 156
Polite by Candlelight, 156
rules review, 158
sign language for manners, 159
Special (recognition) Plate, 161
Speed for Please (rule), 160
Victory Candle, 162
Marker Cap Keeper, 91
Meals on Wheels, 190
Measuring Wall, 150
Memory Boxes, 215

Memory Phrase (for school gear), 21
Mileage Markers, 107
Mini Greenhouses, 116
Mini Mudroom, 224
Mini Museums, 232
Mini Photo Albums, 217
Mission: Lights Out, 47
Mixed-up Animals, 99
Mixed-up family album, 103
Mom-mart, 152
Money Tree, 135
Monstrous Sounds, 50
Monthly Mailings, 183
Mornings
Customized Clock, 15
Doggy Wake-Up Call, 12
Mock Clock, 15
Morning Checklist, 10
Morning Menus, 19
Musical Challenge, 13
Personal Soundtrack, 13
Read-Aloud Routine, 12
Timer in Charge, 14
Mother-Daughter Book Club, 143
Movie Masquerade, 76
Movie Night, Family, 76
Musical Challenge, 13
Musical-note Bingo, 134
My Art Book, 245
Mystery (lunch) Treat, 26

N
Name (ball) Game, 111
Napkin of the Day, 27
Neighborhood Dinner Co-op, 73
New Student Send-off, 210
newspaper clippings, 182
Nightly Check-off, 46
Nighttime Treasure Walk, 78
No-Fear Dinners, 156
Nursing-home Angel, 188

P
Padded (bunk bed) ladder, 236
Painting
Abstract Family Art, 241

Apple Print Shirts, 128
Fabric-Painted Gloves, 101
Finger-Painting Fun, 93
Fun House, 95
Handprint Blanket, 207
Handprint Border, 239
Handprint T-shirt, 170
Heartfelt Bag, 172
Limited Editions, 241
Paint Bottles, 92
Painted Frames on the Wall, 242
Pumpkin Snowman, 129
Rose-colored Windows, 133
Splatter Mat, 93
Stamped Stains (for T-shirts), 101
Terrific Tote, 172
Papa's life board game, 186
Paper Dolls, Homemade, 99
Park-in (garage) Movie, 77
Parties for Charity, 195
Pen-pals Kit, 176
Perfect Place Mats, 40
Perpetual (grocery) List, 32
Personal Binders, 227
Personal Soundtrack, 13
Personalized ink stamp, 166
Personalized math problems, 151
Personalized Portfolios, 245

Photo projects
Classmate Cards, 105
Family Felt Board, 102
Funny Pictures, 102
Mixed-up family album, 103
Photo (first day of school) Sign, 209
Photo (postcard) Mailers, 180
Photo Place Mats, 220
Photo Stories, 186
Photo thank-you, 166

Picky eaters
Adventurous Eater, 45
Cool It (with frozen fruit), 44
Fruit and Veggie Bingo, 44
Picture Labels (for toys), 231
Place Cards with a Twist, 41
Pocket Planner, 11
Polite by Candlelight, 156

Pool on Ice, 123
Postcard Wall, 240
Present for the Postman, 168
Pressed Flower Hangings, 119
Prize (task) Jar, 38
Project Bags, 85
Project Boxes, 88
Pumpkin Snowman, 129
Punch Card for Chores, 35

R
Race Training, 66
Radio Hour, Family, 75
Rain Gutter Bookshelves, 238
Read-Aloud Routine, 12
Reading aloud, 142
Reading Basket for Classroom, 174
Reading resources, 142
Reading Tent, 144
Recipe File of Favorites, 43
Rice Table, Portable, 114
Ring of Postcards, 221
Rock Box, 114
Rose-colored Windows, 133
Rotating Diary, 62
Rotating Menu, 42
Rules review, 158

S
Scarecrow-Making Party, 126
Scavenger Hunt, 60

Schedules, family
Color-Coded Calendar, 28
Daily Flip Cards, 28
Daily (paper) Triage, 29
Weekly meeting, 29

School
After-School Icons, 20
annual getting ready video, 209
Back-to-School Book, 208
Backpack Notes, 20
Bus-stop Bash, 211
Chalkboard Cake, 212
Form Letter (for teachers), 22
Get-to-Know-You (teacher) Tea, 213

Kindergarten Party, 210
Knapsack Neatener, 23
Letter of Introduction, 213
Memory Phrase (for school gear), 21
New Student Send-off, 210
Photo Sign, 208
Science Lab, 149
Seaside Tea Set, 125

Self-esteem
Boss for the Day, 55
Can-do Can, 96
Family Awards Night, 162
Good Fairy, 160
Happy Relationship Day, 54
King for the Day, 200
Life-size Portrait, 96
Rotating Diary, 62
Show and Share, 75
Special Plate, 161
Talking Chair, 64
Together Time, 200
Victory Candle, 162
Self-portrait T-shirt, 171
Sewing Party (for shelter), 193
Shadow-box Mementos, 218
Shared Scrapbook, 178
Show and Share, 75

Siblings
Big Sister Box, 233
Brother Bank, 159
Brotherly Love, 56
Countdown Paper Chain, 206
Handprint Blanket, 207
Kid of the Day, 55
Limited Editions (paintings), 241
Sibling Gift, 201
Sister Book, 56
Sidewalk Chalk Spelling 138
Sign language (for manners), 159
Sister Book, 56
Sleepover Kit, 201
Slumber Party, Family, 80
Sneakers for Kids (donation), 192
Snow Day Box, 132
Snowball Targets, 132
Snowman Bird Feeder, 130
Sounder Snoozing, 50

Special (rules) Dispensation, 38
Special (recognition) Plate, 161
Speed for Please (rule), 160
Splatter Mat, 93
Spring activities
Flower Hunt, 118
Grassroots Stylist, 116
Mini Greenhouses, 116
Pressed Flower Hangings, 119
Wading Pool Garden, 117
Stackable (laundry) Drawers, 246
Stair Assignments, 225
Stamped Stains (for T-shirts), 101
Starry Campout, 81
Sticker Tag, 110
Stickers for blinds, 241
Story Tape, Homemade, 207
Stuffed-animal Hanger, 235
Summer activities
Activity-a-Day Calendar, 120
Beach Golf, 124
Hogwarts Summer Academy, 121
Ice-cream Tasting Party, 123
Lawn-mower Patterns, 122
Pool on Ice, 123
Seaside Tea Set, 125
Tic-tac-toe in the Sand, 125
Summer Survival Kit (for teacher), 175
Sunset drive, 61
Sweet Rewards, 36

T

Table-Setting Tasks, 40
Tabletop Gallery, 244
Tabletop Map, 147
Tackle Box for Hair ties, 248
Talking Chair, 64
Talking Stick, 68
Task Train, 35
Teacher appreciation
Collection of Compliments (T-shirt), 171
Gift Certificate, 173
Handprint (class) T-shirt, 170
Heartfelt Bag, 172
Reading Basket for the Classroom, 174

Self-portrait T-shirt, 171
Summer Survival Kit, 175
Terrific Tote, 172
Ten Items at a Time, 230
Thankful Caterpillar, 65
Thank-yous
coach's thank-you, 169
Day of Thanks, 167
personalized ink stamp, 166
photo thank-you, 166
Present for the Postman, 168
Thank-you Kit, 164
thank-you note brainstorming, 165
thank-you note template, 165
thank-you notes for sponsors, 194
Themed Evenings, 74
Three Good Things, 65
Tickets for the Tube, 30
Tic-tac-toe in the Sand, 125
Time in a Bottle, 219
Timer in Charge, 14
Together (birthday) Time, 200
Toiletries Tote, 248
Token Trade-Off (for TV), 30
Toy Animal Zoo, 86
Toy Storage
Furry Friends Shoe Bag, 235
Mini Museums, 232
Picture Labels, 231
Stuffed-animal Hanger, 235
Three-Shelf Dollhouse, 234
Toy Checkout, 230
Trinket Box, 233
Trash-bag Snowman, 129
Treasure Jar, 109
Trinket Box, 233
Trips as (reading) Treats, 145
T-shirt Quilt, 100
Tube Puppets, 98
TV time
Fun (no-TV) Zone, 31
Tickets for the Tube, 30
Token Trade-Off, 30

U

Under-the-Bed Bins, 247

V

Vacation memories
cameras for the kids, 221
Photo Place Mats, 220
Ring of Postcards, 221
Shadow-box Mementos, 218
Time in a Bottle, 219
Very Crafty Apron, 90
Victory Candle, 162
Videos
Annual getting ready for school video, 209
Everyday Life, 214
growing up video, 204
Video Scrapbook, 214
Volunteering, see *Community Service*

W

Wading Pool Garden, 117
Walking Circle, 67
Wall (alphabet) Stickers, 137
Wallpaper Cutouts, 239
Wall-to-wall (hospital) Visitors, 187
Weather Center, 148
Weekend Plan, 74
Weekly meeting, 29
Week's Worth of Outfits, 16
Wheelbarrow Sandbox, 115
Where-We're-Going (errand) Map, 32
"Whoops" Board, 37
Winter activities
Ice-globe Lanterns, 131
Rose-colored Windows, 133
Snow Day Box, 132
snowball targets, 132
Snowman Bird Feeder, 130
Word Challenge, 140
Word Pitch Game, 139
Workout Routines, 66
Written (lunch choice) Record, 24

Y

Yes Day, 57

Photographers

Susan Andrews: 214 and 237
Susan Barr: 154
Enrico Ferorelli: 236 (bottom)
Peter N. Fox: 72, 80, 109, 110
Andrew Greto: 42, 52, 164, 166, 182, 217, 224, 238 (right), 240, 246 (top), 248 (bottom), 249, and back cover (center)
Ira Gostin/Gostinphoto.com: 239 (top)
Jacqueline Hopkins: 209 and 211
Geoff Johnson: 190
Ed Judice: Front cover (left and right center), 3, 8, 15, 21, 22, 28, 29, 84, 134, 140, 144, 150, 171, 172 (bottom), 173, 174, 185, 222, 225, 226, 231, 238 (left), 239 (bottom), 242, 246 (bottom), 247, 248 (top), and back cover (second one down)
Peter Lacker: 241 (bottom)
Marcy Maloy: Front cover (far right) and 82
Mark Mantegna: 229
Michael McDermott: 149
Niedorf Photography: 192
John Russell: Front cover (left center), 4, and 196
Mary Schjeldahl: 12, 17, 25, 30, 33, 36, 39, 47, 60, 61, 62, 63, 66, 69, 71, 74, 75, 85, 89, 107, 118, 123, 131, 138, 153, 157, 159, 161, 163, 189, 195, 200, 203, 213 (left), and 220

Stylists

Susan Fox, Bonnie Aunchman-Goudreau, Ann Lewis, Sarah Luddick, Karen Quatsoe, Kimberly Stoney, Maryellen Sullivan, and Lynn Zimmerman

Also from **FamilyFun**

***FamilyFun* Magazine:** a creative guide to all the great things families can do together. For subscription information, call 800-289-4849.

***FamilyFun* Boredom Busters:** 365 games, crafts, and activities for every day of the year (Disney Editions, $24.95).

***FamilyFun* Fast Family Dinners:** 100 Kid-friendly recipes your family will love (Disney Editions, $14.95).

***FamilyFun* Family Nights Kit:** fun activities and craft supplies for four stay-at-home nights. (Disney Editions, $18.95).

***FamilyFun* Home:** 250 creative projects and practical tips to make your home truly family-friendly (Disney Editions, $24.95).

***FamilyFun* Vacation Guide Series:** take the vacation your family will remember with our guidebooks, covering New England, Florida, the Mid-Atlantic, the Great Lakes, the Southwest, and California and Hawaii.

***My Great Idea on FamilyFun*.com:** find inspiration and creative tips from other parents — or contribute your own great ideas at FamilyFun.com/mygreatidea